Long Ago a
Eight Traditio

# Long Ago and Far Away

## Eight Traditional Fairy Tales

*Foreword by Marina Warner*

Translated by:
Nigel Bryant, David Carter and
Ann Lawson Lucas

Published by Hesperus Press Limited
28 Mortimer Street, London W1W 7RD
www.hesperuspress.com

This selection first published by Hesperus Press Limited, 2012

'The Slave Girl' and 'Cinderella Cat' translations © Ann Lawson Lucas, 2012

'Little Red Cap', 'The Grandmother's Tale', 'Thumberling', 'Beauty and the Beast'
and 'Undine' translations © David Carter, 2012

'Sleeping Beauty' translation: reprinted in an edited version from *Perceforest: the
Prehistory of King Arthur's Britain*, translated by Nigel Bryant (D.S. Brewer 2011),
by permission of Boydell & Brewer Ltd. © Nigel Bryant 2011

Foreword © Marina Warner, 2012

Designed and typeset by Fraser Muggeridge studio
Printed in Jordan by Jordan National Press

ISBN: 978-1-84391-362-7

# CONTENTS

Jacob and Wilhelm Grimm moved in the circle of Romantic nationalists – musicians, poets and artists – who began collecting folklore in order to discover a German identity; unearthing historical memories and legends, proverbs, superstitions, nostrums, ballads and fairy tales would define their culture retrospectively – and for the future. In the middle of the Napoleonic invasions, this quest was urgent, and the Grimms were struggling to define a specific world view for the German nation which was to emerge and coalesce over half a century after they published the first edition of the classic collection of stories, *Children's and Household Tales*, in 1812. In the final standard edition of 1857, this book has been translated into more languages than any other except the Bible.

The brothers were spurred on especially by men and women of letters who shared an interest in turning away from the universal classical tradition of Greece and Rome towards a popular, vernacular, unlettered store of knowledge. Achim von Arnim and Clemens Brentano, who collected German songs for the anthology *Des Knaben Wunderhorn* (The Young Man's Wonderful Horn) in 1805–8, and Clemens's wife Bettina von Arnim, were avid to hear the tales the brothers were transcribing from the lips of the *Volk*, the people. This was the young men's dream, as they began going around the country gathering stories, resembling the fairy tales' own protagonists picking mushrooms and foraging for kindling in the depths of the forests. Or so they pictured their work. In Marburg, for example, the university town where they were students, they visited the poorhouse where an old woman was celebrated for her repertoire, but they found she didn't want to pass on her lore to the fine young scholars, so the brothers persuaded a little girl to act as go-between.

Several of their informants were not, however, such primary, authentic sources, but educated and well-travelled women (and some men), themselves formed by contacts, cross-currents and migrations. Several of the Grimms' most well-loved fairy tales were told them by Dorothea Wild, Wilhelm's wife, and by friends and contacts of friends, not illiterate peasants or artisans at all. Very soon, the brothers realised that the tales were not *echt* German, could not be marshalled to support a pure, local strain of imagination, but had kith and kin from many elsewheres: the Sleeping Beauty, Red Riding Hood, Cinderella were migrants, blow-ins, border-crossers, tunnellers from France and Italy and more distant territories where earlier and similar stories had been passed on in Arabic and Persian and Chinese and Sanskrit...

It was a vertiginous vision that swallowed the concept of a home culture, and placed in its stead a hubbub of voices, the narrative mêlée of the past jostling to find a place to speak for the present. Folklore scholars later developed a classification system to cover all combinations of plots and motifs, and the argument between the diffusionists, who believe stories travel, and the universalists, who propose a collective unconscious, still carries on. Structuralists like the Russian Vladimir Propp influentially argued there were only this number of stories, or that number of plot devices. It's quite common to hear someone claim that there are only seven stories and all the rest are variations on them. This view can only be maintained by taking a very blunt approach, and novelists pride themselves on innovations and originality. But in the early nineteenth century, the Grimms were rattled by the correspondences and echoes. They tried to purify their findings, and they kept to their story that the stories sprang from the imaginations of the uneducated poor who could not have learned them from books. Wilhelm in particular edited assiduously, changing the first volume to try and eliminate foreign elements, and writing and rewriting the tales, excising some altogether as too French, and adapting others to get closer to a particular local accent and to avoid crudeness, observe sexual taboos, and draw Christian morals.

This Hesperus collection has selected nine alternatives to the classic versions, which give a sense of the liberty of the genre, its general indifference to seemliness, its 'cunning and high spirits', in the phrase of Walter Benjamin, and its inventiveness. The first six stories offer lesser-known, earlier versions of familiar fairy tales from the Grimms' anthology. The medieval romance of 'Perceforêst' is a chivalric predecessor of *Dornröschen* by the Grimms (itself a version of 'La Belle au bois dormant' by Charles Perrault), and reveals the affiliations between the literature of enchantment in the Middle Ages and later, domesticated nursery standards. Giambattista Basile, a mischievous writer of extravagant, baroque Neapolitan fantasy (still not as read as he deserves), included the transgressive 'The Cinderella Cat' and 'The Slave Girl' in his ebullient collection, *The Pentameron, or The Tale of Tales* (1634-6). Two versions of 'Red Riding Hood' follow, the second one of the most vivid orally recorded re-tellings ever captured, earthy and irreverent. The next three tales present different versions of French predecessors (the hero's enemy in the sprightly English pantomimic 'Jack and the Beanstalk' is a close relative of Charles Perrault's comic ogres, while Mme de Villeneuve's unknown, highly digressive romance, 'La Belle et la bête', is far more familiar from the governess Mme de Beaumont's conscious taming of it for pedagogical purposes; the fairy tale, closely inspired by 'Cupid & Psyche' by Apuleius, was re-enchanted by

Jean Cocteau in his 1946 film and by Angela Carter with her gorgeous and perverse 'reformulations' in *The Bloody Chamber* of 1975). The last fairy tale here, 'Undine', by one of the Grimms' compatriots and fellow cultural nationalists, the unlikely soldier de la Motte Fouqué, draws richly on the 'The Tale of Gulnare of the Sea' from the Arabian Nights and blends it with northern folklore about selkies and sea-nymphs. The mysterious enchantress Undine lies behind the heroine of 'The Little Mermaid', by the most brilliant practitioner of the storytelling art, Hans Christian Andersen, a younger contemporary of the brothers Grimm and another Northern European.

A fairy tale is different every time it is told, and takes colour and texture from the context of the telling: while the first Cinderella extant, as told in China in the ninth century, is instantly recognisable as the heroine of the classic story, she has a scholar for a prince, in accordance with the ancient Chinese system of values (books over dosh). It's one of the marks of fairy tale as a genre that the stories' interest isn't exhausted by repetition, reformulation or retelling, but gives pleasure from the endless permutations performed on the original, as in a tune replayed with variations. 'Experience which is passed on from mouth to mouth,' writes Walter Benjamin in his inspired essay, 'The Storyteller', 'is the source from which all storytellers have drawn.' He continues, 'And among those who have written down the tales, it is the great ones whose written version differs least from the speech of the many nameless storytellers.'

The folklorists of the nineteenth century laid too much emphasis on a national *Geist* (spirit) expressed by stories told in a certain language, and their model of oppositions between textual and oral transmission, popular and elite origins, literate writers and illiterate tellers, was starkly schematic and has been superseded. The flow and contraflow between voice and page and back again have been incessant in the history of the literature of enchantment, while performance, from antique oratory to present-day video games, has always conducted such stories from a fixed script to fluid narration in different forms. Two hundred years after the Grimms first published the *Tales*, their work has poured into the sea of stories and fed the streams that flow from it and carried them all over the world. At a crucial moment in literary history, the earnest and scholarly pair acted as keepers of the records, like the scribes whom Caliph Harun al-Rashid commanded, after he'd heard an especially enthralling tale in the great sequence performed nightly by Shahrazad, to write the story down in letters of gold and place it in the state archive. The Grimms set out to capture the national imagination of their country, but time has revealed them to have been unwitting internationalists; they set down stories that have been in movement across borders for centuries, and that once upon a time and far away were entertaining audiences – listeners and readers – and will continue to undergo irrepressible transformations and find themselves occasionally caught by a passing translator, printer and publisher, as here.

– *Marina Warner, 2012*

# Long Ago and Far Away

# SLEEPING BEAUTY

From the French romance *Perceforest*, composed c. 1330–40 (first printed edition Paris, 1528), translated by Nigel Bryant.

*The first written version of the story that has come to be known as 'The Sleeping Beauty' appears in* Perceforest, *a fourteenth-century French romance remarkable not least for its extraordinary length: it is composed of six books, each the length of a substantial novel – the shortest is as long as* Moby Dick. *This rich and fascinating work tells the 'prehistory' of King Arthur's Britain, providing an ancestry for all the major figures in the Arthurian world. It traces Arthur's own bloodline back to Alexander the Great, and here, in the original 'Sleeping Beauty' story, tells of the conception and birth of a child who later proves to be the ancestor of Lancelot. The story begins as a Scottish knight, Troylus, rides in urgent search of his lost love Zellandine.*

Troylus rode through a near-deserted land till he found himself by the sea, where he came upon a ship from Zeeland blown off course by wind and tide. The crew had extraordinary news.

'Zellandine, daughter of our lord Zelland, returned home recently from Britain, and two days later the strangest thing happened: she was sitting with the other maidens when she fell so deeply asleep that she hasn't woken since! All the doctors are powerless to help her.'

Troylus was horrified: he loved Zellandine more dearly than himself. He implored them to take him across to Zeeland, saying: 'I know a lot about medicine thanks to my father – he was one of the finest doctors alive!'

They set sail at once, and put Troylus safely ashore in Zeeland. And that night he took lodging with a lady who told him more about Zellandine's plight: 'She was in her chamber with two of her cousins when she took a distaff laden with flax and started to spin. But she'd barely begun when she lay down, overcome by sleep, and she hasn't woken, drunk or eaten since – though she's lost no weight or colour. Every-one's amazed she's still alive, but they say the goddess Venus, whom she's always served, keeps her in good health.'

Troylus begged to be shown where she was, for he'd do anything in his power to help, and the lady said she'd gladly direct him to her because: 'My son loves her so much that I fear for his life if she dies!'

When Troylus heard he had a rival he was stricken with jealousy. The lady saw his countenance change and guessed the reason; but, clever woman that she was, she didn't show it. Instead she led him to a chamber where, I know not by what art, the moment she left he was suddenly quite lost: he had no recollection of Zellandine – he might as well never have seen her; in fact he was like an idiot, with no memory at all! In his mindless state he suddenly felt the urge to be gone from the room, and climbed through a window and wandered off into the forest. Next day he was in the open fields, where he lost his shoes in the clinging mud and was soaked to the skin by the pouring rain – but he hadn't the wit to be aware of his plight.

Several days later he staggered into the castle of Zellandine's father, the lord Zelland. As he stood gawping like a half-wit at the pictures adorning the walls of the hall, a born fool – a simpleton – of Zelland's household looked at Troylus and suddenly said: 'Come and sit down with the others, master: you'll cure the lovely Zellandine!'

And so saying, he tugged with all his might at Troylus's cloak. Troylus pulled away so sharply that the poor fool tumbled to the floor, but as soon as he was up again he was back to his tugging, trying to pull Troylus over to the doctors who were debating what to do to help their lord's sleeping daughter. He finally gave up and came to Zelland and said: 'Forget these doctors, sir! You only need this fool! He's the one who'll cure your daughter!'

'Be off with you, you simple fellow!' said Zelland, who set little store by his words.

'What? You don't believe me? I promise you she'll never be cured by anyone but him! He's got the remedy!'

Zelland took no notice, but rose and came to Troylus and asked him where he was from. Troylus, his mind altered by herbs or spells, replied so inanely that Zelland took him for a simpleton, and turned back to his doctors. But they could tell him nothing – only that what had happened to his daughter wasn't natural, and that he should lock her in a tower to await the will of the gods, who move in mysterious ways.

Zelland was distressed by their lack of a solution but did as they advised. He had the girl carried to the very top of the tower and laid in a bed, as perfectly prepared as could be; he then had every entrance to the tower blocked up except the topmost window, facing east, in the room where his daughter lay. Then he and his sister went to see her once a day to find out if the gods had taken pity on her – but they always found her in the same state, neither better nor worse.

Then one day Zelland decided to go to a nearby tem ple called the Temple of the Three Goddesses, built long ago by the ladies of the land in honour of the goddess Venus, of Lucina, goddess of childbirth, and of Themis, goddess of destiny; and there he prayed for their mercy on his daughter

Zellandine. Now Troylus, for all his distracted state, was fond of Zelland, and had followed him there; and he chanced to fall asleep in a corner of the temple and Zelland went home without him. And as he slept, about midnight a lady appeared to him and said: 'Arise, knight!'

This lady was of the noblest bearing and wondrous beauty. Her face was very hot and flushed, and her eyes were bright and alluring and seemed on the point of tears – not of grief or anger but of pleasure and excitement. Her head was most elegantly adorned, her shining, almost golden hair arrayed in two tresses; and her garments were green, embroidered with little golden birds. Seeing this glorious lady in his dream, Troylus wondered who she could be and where she was from, for she seemed very forward and had clearly not yet forsaken worldly pleasures. She evidently wanted some response; he thought the least he could do was bid her welcome, so he stood up with courteous words of greeting and asked her who she was. She laughed out loud and said: 'I am the goddess of love, sir knight! I know how to help and guide all true lovers, and because I know you to be a true lover I shall cast off your affliction.'

So saying, she raised her hand and moistened her middle finger with saliva, and dabbed it on his eyes and ears and lips; and in his dream it seemed to him that a veil had been lifted from his sight and his befogged memory was restored to him and he remembered all things past. He peered about as if he'd emerged from darkness into light, and saw the goddess – but she was suddenly gone. A moment later he awoke bewildered, the more so at finding himself alone in the temple, lit only by three lamps burning before the three goddesses. Uncertain how he'd come to be there, he made his way to the temple door – but it was locked fast.

He had to bide his time till morning, when an old man came and opened up. When he saw Troylus he recognised him as Zelland's fool and said: 'What are you doing here, fool? Why didn't you go home yesterday with our lord Zelland?'

'Worthy sir,' Troylus replied, 'I may not be as clever as I might be but I'm not a fool!'

The old man apologised for the word but told Troylus he'd seen him behaving like a simpleton ever since he arrived a week before. Troylus was more than a little puzzled, imagining he'd been in the land just a single night; but the old man insisted it was so and said: 'I don't know if you remember, but the moment he saw you Zelland's fool said to his master: "Here's the doctor who'll cure your daughter!"'

Troylus, struggling to grasp all this, said: 'Now that you remind me of the girl's affliction, I pray you tell me how it came about.'

'Truly, sir,' the old man said, 'there's not a doctor in the land who can explain it. But I'll tell you what the midwives are saying. They have a custom in this land that, when a woman is a week from her confinement, she comes to the temple with a company of other women to make her devotions to the three goddesses who're worshipped here. Then on the day of the delivery they have one of their chambers splendidly prepared, and a table spread with all manner of food and drink. And when the pregnant woman has given birth, the three attendant goddesses go and eat at the table in secret, invisible to all. Each goddess finds her plate laden with all kinds of delicacies, her jug full and her goblet and her knife laid ready. The goddess Lucina has pride of place since she has brought the creature into the world – dead or alive. Next to her sits the goddess Venus, who has her torch ready to fire the child, as soon as it's born, with that vital heat, filling each limb to the child's

7

capacity – be it male or female – so that he or she can put it to good use at the due and appropriate age. And next to her sits Themis, goddess of destiny, who immediately determines the child's life and all that will befall it – bitter or sweet as the goddess chooses. And what the midwives are fearing now is that, at the birth of Zellandine, the goddesses were perhaps not welcomed in the manner they would wish, so that all three – or two or one alone – felt aggrieved, and that may be the cause of the girl's affliction.'

'Indeed,' said Troylus, 'I've heard so much good of the girl that I'm sorry she's so troubled. Please tell me where she is now.'

'She's lying in a strong tower where her father Zelland has had her placed, alone, away from everyone. He's entrusted her to the protection of the gods, for the doctors say medicine's powerless.'

While they were talking Zellandine's aunt – Zelland's sister – arrived at the temple to pray to the three goddesses to have pity on her niece. Troylus, too embarrassed by his wretched state to face her, slipped away and headed into the forest.

As he neared a spring beside a spreading oak, he saw a horse tethered to a lance fixed in the ground, and a shield was hanging from the saddle. They were the very lance and shield he'd brought to that land. And lying on the ground was a knight clad in Troylus's own armour. He was baffled – until he remembered the lady who'd given him lodging and had said a son of hers was in love with Zellandine. Troylus blazed with rage and jealousy; but he was too noble-hearted to recover his arms by treachery or wheedling: it would have to be with the edge of a sword – if only he had a weapon; but what was he to do? He hadn't so much as a stick! Then an idea struck him: he took the shield from the saddle along with the left stirrup, which would make a good and heavy weapon. Just as he did this the knight stood up, ready to ride to the castle to find news of his beloved Zellandine. The moment he saw Troylus he said:

'Who do you think you are, boy? How dare you take my shield and stirrup?'

'I'm one,' said Troylus, 'who claims this shield and the mail on your back in the name of a knight who left them at a lady's house where he lately took lodging. He left there without them – though he's no idea how – and now I challenge you on his behalf!'

'What?' cried the knight. 'You wretched little nobody! You're not worthy to fight me and not equipped to defend yourself!'

He aimed a mighty blow at him, but Troylus blocked it with his shield and whirled the stirrup three times like a sling and struck the knight on the helm with such force that he was completely stunned. Troylus leapt forward and snatched the sword from his grip, then dealt him a second blow with the stirrup that laid him flat on the ground. He threatened to behead him unless he answered his demands. The knight was powerless: he admitted he was the son of the lady who'd given him lodging, and that she'd used the power of certain herbs to deprive Troylus of his memory and left him to wander witless from her house into the forest. Troylus made him agree to go to Zelland, saying: 'Tell him the idiot knight thanks him deeply for the kindness he showed him in his time of need, and say he's sending you as his prisoner to avenge the wrongs that you and your mother did him.'

Then Troylus took back his arms and mounted the knight's horse and set off, leaving him to make his way on foot to surrender to Zelland.

As he rode in urgent search of the castle where Zellandine lay sleeping, Troylus found himself once more near the temple to the three goddesses. He decided to go and pray to Venus for guidance, and knelt before her statue and told her: 'That beautiful girl is my life and my death: if she dies I shall despair! All my joy will be lost and I'll die a shameful death – if any death can be shameful when love is the cause.'

The goddess Venus, who is most merciful and well disposed to lovers who appeal to her for help – and who takes great pleasure in delivering love's ultimate reward – heard his prayers. Suddenly Troylus heard a female voice saying:

Be not troubled, noble knight.
If you've the valour
To enter the tower
Where that noble-hearted beauty
Lies still as stone,
When you pluck from the slit
The fruit that holds the cure,
The girl will be healed.

Troylus was overwhelmed: it seemed that if he could do as the verses said, he would cure Zellandine! But he was frustrated that he didn't understand the meaning of the words, and he cried aloud: 'Ah, noble goddess! You've brought me such comfort! But when I reach the tower, guide me to the slit and teach me how to pluck the fruit and how to use it to cure the girl!'

No sooner had he said this than he heard the same voice answer, saying:

The verses have no need of gloss!
I'll just say this:
Love will find the slit
And Venus, who knows the fruit so well,
Will pluck it:
Nature will see to that!
If you're a man, be on your way!
We don't need all this talking!

Troylus still felt none the wiser, but he left the temple and set off, pondering on the verses from which he could plumb no meaning. All he knew was that he was determined to find the tower.

With the help of an old woman he at last found the way, but when he reached the castle he saw it was protected by deep moats and a raised drawbridge. And the tower in which Zellandine lay was amazingly high, and every door and window had been filled in with solid stones – all except one at the very top, facing east. Troylus saw a messenger riding towards the castle, who confirmed that the girl lay on the topmost storey and said: 'Only her father Zelland goes there: they say he enters the tower by an underground passage. And because he wants the gods to come and cure her he's placed her in a bed way up there – with a window facing east because he has great faith in the god of the sun.'

Not wanting to be seen, Troylus hid in a thicket of alder trees while he pondered how to find a way into the tower. All day he stayed there, fretting. Finally night fell, and his heart and body burned at the thought of the beautiful Zellandine. Made reckless by love, he rode to the edge of the castle moat and plunged in, and Fortune, who tends to favour the brave, saw him safe to the other side. But the walls were solid, impregnable, impossible to scale, and Troylus slumped to the ground in despair and railed against the god of Love, 'Profligate with your promises but the meanest of givers! Were it not for my faith in your dear and merciful mother, the goddess Venus, I'd give up on all your promises!'

Just as he said this there was a brief and violent blast of wind, and a moment later he saw a messenger walking straight towards him over the water of the moat. The astonished Troylus asked him who he was looking for, and the messenger replied:

'Troylus of Royalville. Do you know where I might find him?'

'Well, I'm pretty sure he's in this land, but I wouldn't want to say much more – I don't know who his friends and foes are.'

'Truly,' said the messenger, 'if you knew me as well as I know you, you wouldn't hide his whereabouts, for I can help him more than anyone – in fact, he'll never achieve what he wants without me.'

'Who are you, good sir, who can help him so much?'

'I am who I am,' he replied, 'and what I say is true.'*

Troylus was unsettled by the messenger's words and feared some trickery. 'I wish he were here,' he said, 'so he could hear you and judge if you're telling the truth.'

'Sir, if I'd thought he was somewhere else I wouldn't have come here! There's no point in hiding: I know you're Troylus! And I know you're trying to find a way into this tower at the prompting of the goddess Venus. If you want to get in you'd better talk to me – what the two of you decide to do then is your business!'

* Readers of *Perceforest* would instantly guess that the mysterious figure was Zephir, a shape-changing, Puck-like trickster who (despite being a fallen angel, cast out of Paradise along with Lucifer) serves the interests of several admirable knights in the romance – and indeed the interests of Britain as a whole.

Troylus was as startled by his words as by his crossing of the moat dry-footed. 'Who are you, good sir?' he asked again.

'One,' replied the messenger, 'who can get you into the tower in an instant, in total safety.' Troylus was amazed, but the messenger assured him: 'Just as I crossed the water without wetting my feet, so I'll get you into the tower without a ladder – and down again when it's time.'

Troylus, burning with desire to be with his beloved, agreed to do whatever he said.

'In that case,' said the messenger, 'I'll transport you to where the girl lies. While you're there, follow the urgings of the goddess Venus and then, once midnight's passed and I call to you, come to me at the window and do as I say.'

And thereupon Troylus felt himself swept into the air, and the next thing he knew he was perched, to his astonishment, on the window ledge a hundred cubits* above the ground. He clambered inside the tower and, hardly daring to look for fear it might all be an illusion, peered about the room. And there to one side of the chamber stood a gorgeous bed, worthy of a queen, its curtains and canopy whiter than snow. He was bowled over with excitement: the blood rushed to his cheeks; his whole body was aflame; he was sure it was the bed where the girl lay, ever-sleeping. He couldn't find the courage to approach: like all true lovers, he was bold in thought and a coward in deed! But at last he stepped forward and drew back the curtain and saw, lying there, the one he loved most in all the world. She was stark naked. His heart and legs gave way and he had to sit down on the edge of the bed. When the Love-ruled knight had recovered a little, he heard the girl breathing so gently in her sleep that it was exquisite to hear,

* A cubit was a measurement based on the length of the arm to the elbow – i.e. about half a yard (50 cms).

but he could hardly see her in the dim lamplight. So he lit a candle and placed it at the foot of the bed; then he could clearly see her face, as she slept as sweetly as if she'd fallen asleep that moment, so perfect was the colour of her cheeks. Troylus was more in love with her than ever; and it seemed that if he called to her there'd be nothing to stop her waking, so he leaned close to her ear and whispered:

'Wake, my love, and speak to me!'

But the girl could neither wake nor speak and gave no sign of having heard. He nudged her with his finger but she didn't stir at all, and when Troylus saw that nothing he could say or do would wake her he was most distressed. He gazed at the sleeping girl, beautiful as a goddess, soft, rose-red and lily-white. He couldn't help weeping, and wondered aloud:

'Have you been poisoned or enchanted by someone envious of the gifts and graces bestowed upon you by the Sovereign God – or is it the gods' vengeance for some wrong done by your father and your mother?'

While he lamented and gazed at her beauty, Love summoned him to kiss her, and he said: 'Would you like me to kiss you, girl?'

He was about to do that very thing when Reason and Discretion marched forward and said: 'Sir knight, no man should breach a girl's privacy without her leave, and he certainly shouldn't touch her while she sleeps!'

Hearing this he drew back from her face, so close to his; but Desire was beginning to prick him in earnest, and told him her privacy was no reason to desist – Reason had no place in such matters! – and Honour was not in danger because a kiss could cure all manner of ills: it was especially good at reviving from a swoon or calming a troubled heart. Troylus was delighted with this argument and felt Reason couldn't possibly reply; so he kissed the girl more than twenty times. She didn't stir but she did turn redder; she was clearly fast asleep, but he told himself that since she was changing colour, it was a sure sign she felt something! And seeing her warm flush, she looked so beautiful to him that he couldn't restrain himself: he kissed her countless times and took great pleasure in it – but the pleasure wore off when she didn't respond. Mightily frustrated he said: 'Ah, Venus, goddess of lovers! You promised me that if I found a way inside this tower, Love would point me to the slit that houses the fruit that'll cure the girl! You'll have to show me how to pluck it – I don't know where it grows! Keep your word, noble goddess, for unless the girl recovers, nothing will be more certain than my death!'

Throughout this lamentation he kept gazing at the girl, and he couldn't help kissing her again, she was so beautiful. And while he was accepting these gifts from her lips, the goddess Venus arrived at his side, invisible, and whispered to his heart: 'What a coward you are, knight! You're all alone with this beautiful girl, the one you love above all others, and you don't lie with her!'

He considered these words and decided to act on them. With Venus's flame firing his heart, he felt inspired to throw off his clothes. But Propriety, directed by the god of Love, told him it would be a betrayal to do this: no true lover would harm his beloved! Troylus had second thoughts; and when Venus saw him demur she was more than disappointed with him, and lit her torch and set him so aflame that he was nearly driven wild by the heat. What's more, she made him consider that no faint heart ever won fair lady – and that the girl wouldn't mind what he did, whatever she might pretend! The knight jumped up and was out of his armour and clothes in a second. He dived under the blanket and alongside the girl, who lay there naked, white and soft. Finding himself in this privileged position, Troylus thought no man had ever been as fortunate as he – if only the girl would speak; but she didn't yet: the time had not yet come. And although this took the edge off his joy, he couldn't help answering Venus's urging and had all he wanted of the beautiful Zellandine – including her right to the name of maiden. And it all happened while she was asleep: she didn't stir at all. But then, at the end, she gave a deep sigh, and Troylus was sure she was about to speak. Dumbstruck with alarm he backed away, ready to act all innocent. As he did so, the one who'd brought him there appeared at the window and said: 'Come on, sir knight! Keep your promise and do as you're told: you've done enough for now, and the fruit that'll cure the lovely girl is plucked!'

Troylus jumped up when he heard the call and threw his clothes and armour back on, and came to the window where the one who'd borne him there was waiting. But he was distraught at the thought of leaving and said: 'Oh, why have you come back so soon? You're taking me from the deepest bliss in the world!'

'Never mind that! Stay much longer and you'll be in trouble! Climb on my back and let's go!'

And just as Troylus was clambering on, he heard someone unlocking the chamber door. It was Zelland: while Troylus had been enjoying himself, the candle he'd lit had shone so bright that Zelland had seen it from his bed. He'd hurried along the secret passage and, finding the door to the tower locked, was sure the gods had come to tend his daughter. So he and his sister had climbed to the chamber and seen through a crack in the door that the candle had been snuffed out. The gods, they thought, must have gone, so in they went; and as they entered, Zelland and his sister saw a knight, his arms shining and gleaming in the moonlight, standing on the window ledge, and right outside was a colossal bird; and they saw the knight climb on to the bird's back and throw his legs astride its neck; and the bird beat its wings and took to the air and an instant later had flown from sight. Zelland and his sister gaped in amazement; then Zelland said it must surely have been 'Mars, the god of battles – we're descended from his line, and he came to visit my daughter! You saw how majestically he was borne away!'

They hurried to see how Zellandine was and found her sleeping exactly as before – though her bed was rather rumpled. And Zelland saw her face was paler than before, and said to his sister: 'The god has given my daughter some medicine to cure her! It's taken away that flush she had! She'll recover now, I'm sure of it – thanks to that god who's kin to us!'

When Zelland finally left the chamber he entrusted his daughter to his sister's care. And as she watched a maid putting the bed back in order, she began to wonder whether Mars, the god of battles, might have been rather too familiar with her niece. But she kept these thoughts to herself.

Zellandine remained in bed, exactly as before, for nine whole months without waking, and visited by no one but her aunt.

And then, one evening at the end of the nine months, fair Zellandine gave birth to a handsome son. Just after the delivery her aunt came to visit her as usual and found the lovely child beside his mother, who was still as fast asleep as ever. The lady was utterly amazed – even more so when she saw the newborn child stretching his neck upward as if seeking his mother's breast, and in doing so finding her little finger and starting to suck upon it eagerly. He kept sucking till he began to cough, and the lady took him in her arms and said:

'Ah, you poor little thing! No wonder you're coughing: there won't have been much milk in there!'

At that very moment the girl awoke and started flailing her arms in bewilderment.

'Zellandine, dear niece!' the lady said. 'How are you? Speak to me!'

And Zellandine, hearing her aunt's voice, replied: 'Dear aunt, I was well enough when I went to bed yesterday, but now I've woken sick! What on earth has happened?'

'It was a little before yesterday!' the lady said. 'For nine months – in which you've shown no sign of waking – you've carried this lovely son in your belly, and today you've given birth to him! But I don't know who his father is.'

When the girl heard this and saw the child she was astounded; but she sensed it was probably true and began to weep, unaware that any man had had dealings with her body. Her aunt tried to comfort her, and explained all that had happened: how she'd fallen asleep and been lodged in the tower by her father so that the gods might visit her, and how she believed that Mars, the god of battles and an ancestor of theirs, had sired the child.

'And in so doing he's restored your health, for which you should give him thanks and praise!'

She was also sure she knew the reason why it had happened: she told Zellandine how she'd prepared the food and drink for the three goddesses on the day of her birth, and how one of them, Themis the goddess of destiny, had taken exception to being without a knife for her food. 'And she decreed that your destiny would be such that: "From the first thread of linen she spins from her distaff a shard will pierce her finger and cast her into a sudden sleep, from which she'll never wake till it's sucked out!"' The goddess Venus, her aunt told her, had responded to Themis's ill temper by promising to ensure that it would indeed be sucked from her finger and that all would be made well. And, she said, 'You should take comfort in having given birth to a child sired by such a mighty god as Mars!'

With that, she started rearranging Zellandine's bed. Then suddenly she saw a bird of wondrous shape swoop in through the window: from the breast upward it was in the form of a woman. It landed on the bed where the child lay, took him in its arms, then beat its wings and flew out again, saying: 'Don't worry about the baby!'

# CINDERELLA

'Cinderella Cat', *La Gatta Cennerentola* from *Lo cunto de li cunti* or *Il Pentamerone* (The First Day, Sixth Entertainment), by Giambattista Basile, first published 1634–6, translated by Ann Lawson Lucas.

*Drawing on many precedents and different cultures,* Lo cunto de li cunti *(later also termed 'The Pentameron') was elaborately constructed using a frame narrative along the lines of* The Arabian Nights, *Chaucer's* Canterbury Tales, *Boccaccio's* Decameron *and Straparola's* The Delightful Nights. *The setting is a prince's court where, over the course of five evenings, his guests recount the tales of 'Cinderella Cat' and 'The Slave Girl' among many others, thus forming an early European collection of stories from oral sources.*

The listeners had heard the tale of the flea and the foolish king in silence, broken next by Antonella in the following manner.

In the ocean of malice, Envy always mistakes poison gas for air bubbles, and when she hopes to see another drown, finds herself either underwater or else dashed on a rock. This happened to certain envious girls whose story I have it in mind to tell you.

Once upon a time, then, there was a widower prince who had a daughter so dear to him that he saw everything through her eyes. He gave her an excellent teacher for her needlework, who taught her chain-stitch, open-work, drawn-thread work and hem-stitch, while showing her more affection than one can describe. But the father married again and his malicious, ill-tempered, wicked new wife immediately took against her stepdaughter, eyeing her cruelly, scowling and making ugly faces at her, to such an extent that she would jump with fright. So the poor child often lamented her ill-treatment by her stepmother when talking to her teacher, saying: 'Dear God, if only you could be my little mother, you who are so kind and loving to me.' In fact she repeated this refrain so often that the governess began to get a bee in her bonnet and, led astray by Old Nick, she ended by saying: 'If you really want to pursue this madcap idea, I will be your mother, and you will be the apple of my eye.' She was about to go on when Zezolla (for this was the name of the girl) said: 'Forgive me if I'm interrupting. I know that you're fond of me, so enough of that, keep your peace: I'm new to this, so teach me the means: you write, I'll sign.' 'Well then,' replied the governess, 'be a good girl and pay attention, and manna will fall from heaven. When your father goes out, tell your stepmother that you do not want to spoil the dress you have on, and would like one of those old garments that are kept in the big chest in the closet. She would be glad to see you covered in rags and tatters, and will open the chest, saying, "You hold the lid." You must hold it while she rummages inside, and then let it fall suddenly so that it breaks her neck. Once it's done, you know that your father would print fake banknotes to keep you happy so, when he's giving you a hug, beg him to take me as his wife; then you'll be happy and you'll be the light of my life.'

After she had listened to the plan, every hour seemed like a thousand years to her until she had carried out in full the instructions of her governess. Once the period of mourning for the stepmother's demise was over, she began to test the ground with her father about marrying the teacher. At first the prince thought it a joke, but his daughter so often followed a parry with a thrust that in the end he took his daughter at her word and, amid great festivity, made the governess Carmosina his wife. Now while they were disporting with each other, Zezolla went to a little balcony in her house and a lovely dove flew on to the wall nearby, saying, 'When you desire something, send to ask the Fairies' dove in the island of Sardinia, and it will be yours at once.'

For five or six days the new stepmother lavished all manner of caresses on Zezolla, sitting her at the best seat at table, giving her the best treats, and dressing her in the finest gowns. But after only a little while, the service that Zezolla had performed was forgotten and vanished into thin air (what a sorry soul is an evil mistress's!) and she began to push forward six daughters of her own, having kept them hidden until then, and so worked on her husband to hold her children dear that his own daughter fell from his affections. So from yesterday's orphan she became today's pauper, and found herself demoted from great hall to scullery, from four-poster to chimney corner, from sumptuous gold and silk to dishcloths, from the sceptre to the spit. Not only did she change her state, but even lost her name, and instead of Zezolla was known as Cinderella Cat.

It happened that the prince had to go to Sardinia on affairs of state, and he asked each of his stepdaughters in turn – Imperia, Calamita, Shiorella, Diamante, Colommina, Pascarella – what they would like him to bring back for them. Some wanted a sumptuous gown, some a fascinating head-dress, some cosmetics for the face, some playthings to pass the time, each wanted something different. Finally, almost as a joke, he said to his daughter: 'And you, what would you like?' And she said, 'Nothing else, except that you remember me to the Fairies' dove and ask her to send me something. And if you should forget, may you be unable to go forwards or backwards. Bear in mind what I'm saying to you: on your head be it.'

The prince departed and transacted his business in Sardinia; he acquired what his stepdaughters had requested and Zezolla slipped his mind. However, embarked once more aboard ship, with the sails unfurled, it proved impossible to leave the harbour, and it seemed that the vessel was being impeded by the remora. All but in despair, the master of the ship fell asleep through exhaustion, and in a dream saw a Fairy who said to him: 'Do you know why you can't get the ship to leave port? It's because the prince who is travelling with you has failed to keep his promise to his daughter, remembering everything except what he owed to his own flesh and blood.' Once he was awake, the master recounted his dream to the prince who, covered in confusion at his omission, made his way to the Fairies' grotto and, commending his daughter to them, explained that she was in need of something. Lo and behold, there stepped forth from the cavern a beautiful young woman, as striking as a standard-bearer, who said she thanked his daughter for her remembrance, and bade her rejoice in her love for her. So saying, she gave him a date palm, a mattock, a little golden bucket and a silken cloth, explaining that the tree was for planting and the other items were for its cultivation.

Marvelling at this present, the prince took leave of the Fairy and proceeded towards his own country, where he gave everything requested to his stepdaughters, and then presented his own daughter with the Fairy's gift. She jumped for joy and planted the date palm in a fine pot; she cared for it, watered it, and with the silken cloth both morning and night she dried it, so that in four days it had grown to the stature of a woman, whereupon there stepped forth a Fairy, saying: 'What is it that you desire?' At this Zezolla explained that she longed to go out sometimes, though without her sisters knowing. The Fairy answered her, 'Every time that you fancy it, come to the pot, and say:

*Oh my golden date palm,*
*With the golden hoe I have cared for you,*
*With the golden pail I have watered you,*
*With the silken cloth I have dried you;*
*Disrobe yourself and dress me!*

'And when you want to undress once more, change the last line and say, "Disrobe me and dress yourself".'

Now one day, which was a festival, all the governess's daughters had left the house, blooming, painted and daubed, all beribboned and trimmed with little bells and furbelows, all perfumed and flowery, with roses and nosegays; so Zezolla ran straight to the pot to say the Fairy's magic words, whereupon she was clothed like a queen and placed on a white steed with twelve fine and dandy pages, and she went where her sisters were. Their eyes watered with envy at the beauty of this lovely dove. As fate decreed, the king himself came to the same place and, when he had seen the extraordinary beauty of Zezolla, he was instantly enchanted by it, and commanded his most trusted servant to inform himself about this lovely creature, who she was and where she lived. The servant set about following in her very footsteps, but she – aware of the trap – threw down a handful of golden coins which she had obtained from the date palm for this purpose. Fired with desire for the shining pieces, he paused to gather them up, forgetting to follow the white steed which swiftly reached the house. There Zezolla undressed in the manner learnt from the Fairy, whereupon those harpies, her sisters, soon returned and, so as to hurt her feelings, told her all about the fine things they had seen.

Meanwhile the servant returned to the king and told him about the coins; the king flew into a great rage and said that for a paltry pittance he had sold out on his master's pleasure and that, at the next festival, he must make it his business to find out who the lovely girl was, and where such a pretty bird might be housed. Bedizened and beribboned, the sisters all went out for the next festivity, leaving the despised Zezolla by the hearth. Straight away she ran to the date palm, repeating the usual words, when lo and behold a group of maidens appeared, one with a mirror, one with a pitcher of pumpkin water, one with curling tongs, one with the rouge, one with a comb and one with pins, and others with garments and earrings and necklaces. When they had made her as glorious as the sun, they put her into a carriage drawn by six horses and accompanied by liveried footmen and pages. She drove to the same place as before and there provoked wonder in the hearts of the sisters and fire in the breast of the king.

But on her departure with the servant behind her, to stop him following her home, she threw down a handful of pearls and jewels, whereupon this fine man took a few, they being too good to miss, and so she had time to hurry back and change her clothes in the usual manner. With a hangdog expression the servant returned to the king, who said: 'By the souls of my dear departed, if you don't find that girl, I'll have you thrashed and I'll give you as many kicks on your backside as you have hairs in your beard.' The next festivity came along and, once the sisters were out of the house, Zezolla went as usual to the date palm, repeated the enchanted song, and was dressed superbly and placed in a golden carriage, with so many attendants round her that she might almost have been a courtesan, arrested while out driving and surrounded by gendarmes. Once she had excited envy in the sisters, she departed, and this time the king's servant attached himself to the carriage by means of a double rope. She, seeing that he was cheek by jowl with her, called 'Faster, coachman', and the carriage set off at a furious pace; the speed was so great that there fell from her foot the most exquisite slipper that you could ever see.

The servant, unable to match the coach which was flying along, picked up the slipper from the ground and took it to the king, telling him what had happened. Taking it in his hand, the king said, 'If the footings are so lovely, what must the superstructure be like? Oh beauteous sconce that held the candle which destroys me! Oh tripod of the lovely cauldron where my life is boiling! Oh charming cork attached to the hook and line of Love which has caught my soul! Behold, I embrace you and I hold you, and if I cannot reach the stem, I shall adore the roots, and if I cannot have the capital, I shall kiss the pillar! First a white foot was imprisoned here, and now a gloomy heart is ensnared; through you the tyrant of my life stood inches taller, and through you the sweetness of this life increases just as much, while I have and hold you.'

This said he called his scribe, and ordered a fanfare, and *tan-ta-rah* he had it proclaimed that all the women in the land were to present themselves at a festival and banquet that he had decided to give. And when the appointed day arrived, oh my goodness what masticating and what celebrating there was! Where had all the cakes and pastries come from? Whence came the casseroles and meatballs, whence the spaghetti and the ravioli? It was enough to feed an army. All the women came, noble and humble, rich and poor, old and young, lovely and ugly, and the well-groomed king, after proposing the toast, started to try the slipper on the feet of each of his guests in turn to see which it fitted to perfection, so that he could know from the shape of the slipper who it was he was seeking. But not finding a foot to fit it, he began to despair. However, having silenced everyone, he said: 'Come back tomorrow to make your penitence with me once again; but, if you love me, do not leave any woman at home, whoever she may be.' Then the prince said: 'I have a daughter who always keeps to the hearth, being pitiable and unworthy, who does not merit a seat at your table.' The king said, 'Let her be at the top of the list, for that is my wish.'

So they all departed and returned the next day, and along with Carmosina's daughters came Zezolla; as soon as the king saw her, he fancied she was the one he desired, but he kept his thoughts to himself. Then, after the feasting came the slipper test and, as soon as it approached Zezolla's foot, the slipper darted of its own accord to the foot of that pretty darling love, like iron filings flying to a magnet. As soon as he saw this, the king ran to embrace her and, seating her beneath a canopy, he placed a crown on her head, commanding all to make their bows and curtsies to her as their queen. Seeing this, the sisters, green with envy and unable to stomach the display of their breaking hearts, slunk off home to mother, admitting in spite of themselves that

*Only a madman challenges destiny.*

# SNOW WHITE

'The Slave Girl', *La Schiavottella* from *Lo cunto de li cunti* or *Il Pentamerone* (The Second Day, Eighth Entertainment), by Giambattista Basile, first published 1634-6, translated by Ann Lawson Lucas.

*Basile brings together stories from both Classical and Oriental sources, as well as from the oral tradition, by embedding them in a framing narrative in which each tale is told by a different teller as entertainment at a royal court. Elements of 'The Slave Girl' prefigure at least three well-known fairy tales in their modern forms: the glass coffin reappears in 'Snow White'; the deathlike state of the girl cursed by a fairy when young is reminiscent of ' The Sleeping Beauty'; the locked and forbidden room, investigated by a curious wife, reappears in 'Bluebeard'.*

The Prince turned to Paola and asked her to tell her tale; at first she licked her lips a lot and scratched her head, and then she began.

To tell the truth jealousy is a very bad failing; it's a fit of vertigo that makes your head spin, a fever that burns in your veins, a numbness that chills the limbs, a dysentery that racks the whole body, a misery indeed that makes you sleepless, sours your food, disturbs your peace and disrupts your life: it is a serpent that bites, a woodworm that gnaws, a gall that poisons, snow that freezes, a nail that pierces and divorces you from the pleasure of love, spoils the sport of lovemaking, and in the ocean of the delights of Venus it batters you with its thunderbolts. Nothing good ever comes of it, as you will admit when you hear the tale that follows.

Once upon a time there was a baron of the Black Wood who had an unmarried sister. She always went out to play in the garden with the other girls of her age; one day they found a lovely rose bush in full bloom and they made a pact that the girl who could jump clean over it, without touching so much as a leaf, should win a prize. Then many of the girls leapt across, straddling it, but all of them touched it, and not one jumped clear. When it was Lilla's turn, who was the sister of the baron, she gave herself a slight advantage, standing back to take a run at it, and she leapt right over the top; but, knocking off one leaf, she was so quick and clever that, in the twinkling of an eye, she had snatched it from the ground and swallowed it, so winning the wager.

Only three days had gone by when she felt herself to be pregnant and she nearly died of grief, knowing full well that she had not engaged in either intrigues or dalliances. As she could not understand how it was that her belly was swelling, she ran off to see certain Fairy friends of hers; they told her to be in no doubt, for the cause of her condition was the rose leaf that she had swallowed. Hearing this, Lilla did what she could to hide her belly, and when the time came to offload her burden, she gave birth in secret to a lovely little girl. She named her Lisa and sent her to the Fairies, each of whom gave her a charm of her own, but the last one, running to see the baby, twisted her foot so disastrously that, in her pain, she cursed her, saying that at seven years old, while her mother was combing her hair, the comb would be forgotten, stuck in her head among the curls, and she would die of it.

When the time arrived and the curse came true, the anguished mother, despairing at this tragedy, lamented bitterly, and enclosed her in seven crystal caskets, one inside the other, and placed her in the most distant room of the palace, keeping the key to herself. But her grief at the occurrence soon brought her to death's door and, summoning her brother, she said to him, 'Brother mine, I feel the hook of death dragging me little by little, therefore it is to you that I leave all my belongings, for you to keep or dispose of as you please. But you must give me your word only that you will never open that last room in the house, and will always keep the key safe in your desk.' Her brother, who loved her greatly, gave his promise, and she at once said, 'Farewell, the time has come.'

However, some years later, now married, this lord was invited to a hunting-party, and so entrusted the house to his wife, begging her above all not to open the room whose key he kept in his desk. Nevertheless, no sooner was his back turned, than she – prompted by suspicion, driven on by jealousy, and eaten up with curiosity (a woman's first endowment) – took the key and unlocked the room; opening the caskets, through which she could see a glimmer of the girl, she found a creature who seemed asleep: she had grown to the stature of a woman and the caskets had increased in size with her. The jealous woman, seeing her loveliness, exclaimed, 'Well, upon my life! You can't keep out the enemy within! No wonder he was determined to keep the room locked and the false god he worshipped hidden in the caskets!' So saying, she grabbed her by the hair and dragged her out, and so it was that the comb fell to the floor and the girl came to life, crying out, 'Mother, oh mother!' 'Wretch, I'll give you mother – and father too!' replied the baroness, who – bitter as a slave, angry as a bitch with pups, poisonous as a snake – at a stroke cut off the girl's hair, gave her a thrashing with the switch, and dressed her in rags. Every day she heaped blows on her head, blacked her eyes, bruised her face, and gashed her mouth so that it looked as if she'd been eating raw pigeons.

When the husband came home and saw how badly treated this girl was, he asked who she was; his wife told him that she was a slave, sent to her by an aunt, and that, as she was fit for nothing else, it was necessary to beat her all the time. When the occasion arose for the lord to go out to a fair, he asked everyone in the house, including even the cats, what they would like him to buy for them; when they had all chosen one thing or another, he finally came to the slave girl. But his wife, not behaving like a Christian, said, 'That's right, lump this thick-lipped slave in with the rest, and let's all be brought down to her level; I'm sure we'd all like the luck to piss in a urinal; leave her alone, for pity's sake, and stop paying attention to such an ugly brute!' All the same, the baron, who was courteous, wanted the slave girl to request something, and she said: 'I don't ask for anything other than a doll, a knife and a pumice stone; and if you should forget, may you not be able to cross the first river that you come to on your journey.'

When the baron had bought all the things except those requested by his niece, and wanted to cross the river which carried stones and trees from the mountains to the shore, for the building of fearsome foundations and wondrous walls, it turned out to be impossible for him to ford the flow. Thus he remembered the slave girl's spell, turned back and carefully obtained everything. At home once more, he distributed his purchases one by one. With her little objects, Lisa retreated to the kitchen and, placing the doll before her, she began to weep and tremble, recounting all the story of her travails to that bundle of rags, as if it were a real person she was addressing; but seeing that it did not respond, she took the knife and sharpened it on the pumice stone, saying, 'I tell you, if you don't answer, I will plunge this in, and that will end the fun!' And the doll, little by little swelling up like the bagpipes when the piper blows, finally answered, 'All right, I have understood you better than a deaf person!'

Now while this music continued for a number of days, the baron, whose study was on the other side of the kitchen wall, by chance hearing this same refrain, put his eye to the keyhole and saw Lisa telling the doll all about her mother's leap over the rose bush, her eating of the leaf, her giving birth, the spell put on her, the curse of the fairy, and all the rest about the comb on her head, her death, her enclosure in the seven caskets placed in the room, her mother's death, the legacy of the key left to the brother, his departure to the hunt, his wife's jealousy, the opening of the room against his orders, the cutting of her hair, her treatment as a slave and the many, many tortures inflicted on her. So saying and weeping, she begged, 'Answer me, little doll, otherwise I shall kill myself with this knife!' And sharpening it on the pumice stone, she tried to plunge it into herself, when the baron, kicking open the door, took the knife from her hand. Listening again more carefully to the story, he embraced her as his niece, and took her away from the house to a relative of his so that she could recover somewhat, for she had become wasted as a result of the harsh treatment inflicted by that cruel Fury. A few months passed and, when she had become as lovely as a goddess, he brought her home and explained to everyone that she was his niece. After he had given a great banquet, and the tables were cleared, he made Lisa tell the story of all the troubles she had borne and the cruelties of his wife, a tale which made all the guests weep. Then he sent his wife away to the house of relatives, and gave his niece a handsome husband of her own heart's desire. So it was that she bore witness to the fact that

*Heaven rains favours on you*
*When you least expect it.*

33

# LITTLE RED RIDING HOOD

*Le petit chaperon rouge* from *Histoires ou contes du temps passé, avec des moralités. Contes de ma mère l'Oye* by Charles Perrault, first published 1697, translated by David Carter.

*Rather than 'mère L'Oye', English-speaking readers will be more familiar with the equivalent term 'Mother Goose' tales, in both cases, a fictional character serving as purported author of collected fairy tales.*

Once upon a time there was a little village girl, the prettiest who had ever been seen. Her mother adored her and her grandmother adored her even more. This old woman had a little red cap made for her, which suited her so well that everywhere she went people called her Little Red Cap.

One day when her mother had baked some round cakes, she said to her, 'Go and see how your grandmother's getting on, because I heard that she was ill. Take her a cake and this little pot of butter.' Little Red Cap set off at once to go to her grandmother, who lived in another village. Passing through a wood she met Master Wolf, who really felt like eating her, but did not dare because of some woodcutters who were in the forest. He asked her where she was going. The poor girl, who did not know that it was dangerous to stop and listen to a wolf, said to him, 'I'm going to see my grandmother, to take her a cake and a little pot of butter from my mother.'

'Does she live very far away?' asked the wolf.

'Oh yes,' said Little Red Cap, 'it's beyond the mill that you can see far over there, in the first house of the village.'

'Well,' said the wolf, 'I want to go and see her too. I'll go off along this path, and you go along that path, and we'll see who gets there sooner.'

The wolf started to run with all his might by the shortest path, and the little girl went by the longest path, enjoying herself gathering hazelnuts, chasing butterflies, and making bouquets of the little flowers that she came across. It did not take the wolf long to get to the grandmother's house and he knocked: Knock! Knock! 'Who's there?' came a voice. 'It's your little grand-daughter, Little Red Cap,' said the wolf disguising his voice, 'and I'm bringing you a cake and a little pot of butter from my mother.' The grandmother, who was in bed because she felt a little unwell, called out to him 'Pull the peg, and the latch will fall.' The wolf pulled the peg and the door opened. He jumped on to the old woman and ate her up in next to no time, for he had not eaten for more than three days. Afterwards he closed the door and went to lie down in the grandmother's bed, and waited for Little Red Cap, who some time after came to knock on the door: Knock! Knock! 'Who's there?' came a voice. Little Red Cap, when she heard the deep voice of the wolf, was at first afraid but, thinking that her grandmother had caught a cold, she replied, 'It's your granddaughter, Little red Cap, and I'm bringing you a cake and a little pot of butter from my mother.' The wolf called out to her, softening his voice a little, 'Pull the peg, and the latch will fall.' Little Red Cap pulled the peg and the door opened. When he saw her coming in, the wolf hid under the blanket on the bed and said to her, 'Put the cake and the little pot of butter on the chest and come and lie down next to me.' Little Red Cap got undressed and went to get into the bed, where she was very surprised to see what her grandmother looked like in her nightdress. She said to her, 'Grandmother, what big arms you have!'

'All the better to embrace you with, my little girl,' he replied.

'Grandmother, what big legs you have!'

'All the better to run with, my child,' he replied.

'Grandmother, what big ears you have!'

'All the better to hear with, my child,' he replied.

'Grandmother, what big eyes you have!'

'All the better to see, my child,' he replied.

'Grandmother, what big teeth you have!'

'They're to eat you up with!' And as he said these words the wicked wolf jumped onto Little Red Cap and ate her up.

From *Le conte de la mère-grand*, oral version first recorded around 1870, and recorded in writing by Paul Delarue in 1951, translated by David Carter.

Translator's note: *In some of the recorded oral versions the wolf is referred to as an ugly or horrible man. By this storyteller it was referred to in all but one sentence as 'le bzou' which is a corrupt form of an old word for 'werewolf'. This version was collected by Achille Millien around 1870 and published by Paul Delarue (1886–1956).*

There was a woman who had made some bread. She said to her daughter: 'Take this nice hot loaf and a bottle of milk to your grandmother.' And so the little girl set off. At the junction of two paths she met the werewolf, who said to her: 'Where are you going?'

'I'm taking a nice hot loaf and a bottle of milk to my grandmother.'

'What path are you taking?' asked the werewolf, 'the one with the needles or the one with the pins?'

'The one with the needles' said the little girl.

'Oh well, I'll take the one with the pins.'

The little girl enjoyed herself picking up the needles.

And the werewolf arrived at the grandmother's house, killed her, and put her flesh in the chest and a bottle of her blood on the ledge of the sink.

The little girl arrived and knocked at the door.

'Push the door,' said the werewolf. 'It is barred with a bale of damp straw.'

'Hallo Grandmother, I'm bringing you a nice hot loaf and a bottle of milk.'

'Put them in the chest, my child. Take the meat which is

in there and the bottle of wine which is on the ledge of the sink.

After she ate, a little female cat said to her:

'Bah!… The bitch!… Look at her eating the flesh and drinking the blood of her grandmother.'

'Get undressed, my child,' said the werewolf, 'and come and lie down next to me.'

'Where should I put my apron?'

'Throw it in the fire, my child. You won't need it any more.'

She also asked him where she should put all her clothes, her corset, her dress, her petticoat and her stockings. And the wolf replied, 'Throw them in the fire, my child. You won't need them any more.'

When she was lying down, the little girl said:

'Oh grandmother, how hairy you are!'

'It's to warm myself up, my child!'

'Oh grandmother, how big your nails are!'

'It's so I can scratch myself better, my child!'

'Oh grandmother, what big shoulders you have!'

'It's so that I can carry my bundle of wood better, my child!'

'Oh grandmother, what big ears you have!'

'It's so I can hear better, my child!'

'Oh grandmother, what big nostrils you have!'

'It's so I can take my snuff more easily, my child!'

'Oh grandmother, what a big mouth you have!'

'It's so I can eat you better, my child!'

'Oh grandmother, how I'm longing to go outside!'

'Do it by the bed, my child!'

'Oh no, grandmother, I want to go outside!'

'Very well, but not for long.'

The werewolf attached a woollen thread to her foot and let her go.

When the little girl was outside, she fixed the end of the thread to a plum tree in the yard. The werewolf became impatient that no one was answering him. He jumped down from the bed and saw that the little girl had run away. He followed her, but he arrived at her house just at the moment when she was going inside.

# HANSEL AND GRETEL

From *Le petit poucet* in *Histoires ou contes du temps passé, avec des moralités. Contes de ma mère l'Oye* by Charles Perrault first published in 1697, translated and abridged by David Carter.

*The title means 'Little Thumb' and has sometimes been translated as 'Tom Thumb', but this leads to confusion with a different tradition of tales in English.*

Once upon a time there was a woodcutter and his wife, who had seven children, all of them boys. The oldest was only ten years old and the youngest was only seven. People were surprised that the woodcutter had had so many children in such a short time, but his wife did not waste any time and never did less than two things at once. They were very poor and their seven children were a great bother to them, because not one of them could earn his own living. What grieved them even more was that the youngest was very delicate and did not speak a word, and they took for stupidity what was a sign of his good disposition. He was very small, and when he came into the world he was scarcely bigger than a thumb, which is why he was called Thumberling. This poor child was the whipping boy of the house, and he was always the one to be blamed. However he was the most shrewd and the most sensible of all the brothers, and if he spoke little he listened a lot.

There was one very distressing year, when the famine was so great that the poor couple resolved to get rid of their children. One evening when the children had gone to bed and the woodman was by the fire with his wife, he said to her, his

41

heart gripped with anguish, 'As you well know we can't feed our children any more. I could not bear to see them dying of hunger before my eyes, and I have resolved to take them to the forest tomorrow and lose them, which will be very easy, as, while they are enjoying themselves doing up bundles of firewood, we only have to run away without them seeing us.'

'Oh!' exclaimed the woodcutter's wife, 'Could you really take your children off and lose them?'

In vain did her husband remind her of their great poverty: she could not agree to it. She was poor but she was their mother. However, after considering what suffering it would cause her to see them dying of hunger, she agreed to it, and went to bed in tears.

Thumberling heard everything they said, for having heard while lying in his bed, that they were discussing some problems, he had got up quietly and slipped under his father's stool, so that he could listen to them without being seen. He went back to bed and could not sleep for the rest of the night, thinking about what he should do. He got up early in the morning, and went to the bank of a stream, where he filled his pockets with little white pebbles, and then returned to the house. They set off, and Thumberling did not reveal to his brothers any of the things that he knew. They went into a very dense forest, where at a distance of ten feet you could not see each other. The woodcutter began to cut some wood and the children collected some small branches to make bundles of firewood. When the father and mother saw that they were busy with their work, they wandered away from them without being noticed, and then suddenly ran off by a little diverging path. When the children realised that they were alone, they started to shout and cry as hard as they could. Thumberling let them cry, because he knew well enough how to get back to the house, for as they had walked along he had dropped along the path the little white pebbles which he had in his pockets. So he said to his brothers, 'Don't be afraid, brothers, Mother and Father have left us here, but I will take you back home. Just follow me.' They followed him and he led them back to their house by the same path by which they had come into the forest. They did not dare to go in, but placed themselves close to the door so that they could hear what their father and mother were saying.

At the very moment when the woodcutter and his wife arrived back home, the Lord of the Village sent them ten écus that he had owed them for a long time, and which they had given up all hope of getting back. This gave them new life, for the poor couple were dying of hunger. The woodcutter sent his wife to the butcher's shop straightaway. As she had not eaten for a long time, she bought three times as much meat as was necessary to make supper for two people. When they had eaten their fill, the woodcutter's wife said, 'Alas, where are our poor children now! They could have eaten well from what we have left. But it was you, Guillaume, who wanted to get rid of them. I said that we would repent it. What are they doing in the forest now? Oh God, wolves have probably eaten them up already. It's inhuman of you to have got rid of your children in that way!' Finally the woodcutter lost his patience, because she repeated more than twenty times that they would repent what they had done, and that she had told him so. He threatened to beat her, if she did not shut up. The woodcutter was probably even angrier than his wife, but she kept on at him about it, and he had a disposition like many other men who prefer women who speak well, but who find them very bothersome when they are always in the right. The woodcutter's wife was full of tears. 'Alas, where are my children now, my poor children?'

And once she said it so loudly that when they heard her, the children, who were outside the door, all started to cry out together, 'We're here, we're here!' She ran quickly to open the door for them, and embracing them she said, 'How pleased I am to see you again, my dear children. You must be weary, and you must be hungry. And you, Pierrot, how muddy you are. Come and let me wash you.' Pierrot was the eldest son, whom she loved more than all the others, because he was a little red-haired and she herself was a little red-haired.

They sat down at the table and ate with an appetite which pleased their mother and father, whom they told about the fear they had felt in the forest, talking all together most of the time. The good couple were delighted to have their children with them again, and this joy lasted only as long as the ten écus lasted. But when the money was used up, they relapsed into their former state of grief, and resolved to get rid of the children again, but to make sure they did not fail, they would take them further than the first time. They were not able to talk about it very secretly, so they were overheard by Thumberling, who worked out how to overcome the problem as he had done the first time. But although he got up early in the morning to go and collect some small pebbles, he could not carry out the task, because he found the door of the house double-locked. He did not know what to do, but when the woodcutter's wife gave them each a piece of bread for their lunch, it occurred to him that he could use his bread instead of the pebbles, by throwing crumbs from it along the paths they followed, and so he put it into his pocket. Their father and mother led them to the thickest and darkest place in the forest, and as soon as they were there, they managed to evade them and left them there. Thumberling was not very worried, because he believed he could find his way again by means of the bread which he had strewn in every place which they passed. But he was really surprised when he could not find a single crumb. The birds had come down and eaten them all. This made them greatly distressed, for the more they walked the more they lost their way, and went further into the forest. Night came and a great wind arose, which made them terribly frightened. They thought they could hear all around them the howling of wolves who were coming to eat them. They scarcely dared talk to each other or turn their heads. There was a sudden downpour of rain which soaked them to the skin. They slipped at every step and fell down into the mire, from which they pulled themselves out again all covered in mud, not knowing what to do with their hands. Thumberling climbed to the top of a tree to see if he could discover anything. After having turned his head in all directions he caught sight of a faint light like that of a candle, but it was far beyond the forest. He came down from the tree, and when he was on the ground he could not see it any more, which distressed him. But after walking for some time with his brothers in the direction in which he had seen the light, he saw it again as they came out of the wooded area. They finally arrived at the house where the candle was, not without several moments of fear, for often they lost sight of it, which happened whenever they went down into some hollows. They knocked on the door, and an old woman opened it to them. She asked them what they wanted, and Thumberling told her that they were poor children who had got lost in the forest and asked her to be kind enough to let them sleep there. The woman, seeing that they were all so good-looking, started to cry and said to them, 'Alas, my poor children, do you know where you have come? Don't you know that this is the house of an ogre who eats little children?'

'Alas, Madam,' replied Thumberling, shaking with all his might, as were his brothers, 'What shall we do? It's certain that the wolves in the forest won't fail to eat us tonight, if you won't let us stay with you. That being the case we would prefer to be eaten by this gentleman, and perhaps he will take pity on us, if you would be so kind as to beg him.'

The ogre's wife, who thought she would be able to hide them from her husband until the next morning, let them come in and took them to warm themselves by a good fire, for there was a whole sheep on a spit for the ogre's supper...

*The story continues with accounts of the ogre's eating habits, his seven ugly daughters, how the seven brothers escaped but were pursued by the ogre in his seven-league boots, and how Thumberling acquired the boots and went back to the ogre's house to take away all his treasures and return laden with them to his parents' home.*

# JACK AND THE BEANSTALK

From *Round About Our Coal Fire: Or Christmas Entertainments*, first published 1734.

*Round About Our Coal Fire was originally published as an eighteenth-century chap-book (a pamphlet-style publication featuring collected tales, nursery rhymes, poetry). Such books were an important vehicle for the dissemination of entertainment, popular culture and history among common people.*

Gaffer Spriggings, who was an acute old farmer, who could leer of one eye and crack a joke, began to tell about a comic lad of his family, of the name of Spriggins, for he admired everyone of his name, because he had no children of his own; and this boy's name was Jack, as we shall call him now.

Good folks, there never was such a dirty, lazy, tatter-de-mallion* dog as Jack in the world; he was elevated in his garret of nights, and had the curse of small beer in his kitchen of days, with an enchantress for his grandmother and companion. When I mention this apartment, I ought in justice to let you know that the house was no more than a hovel or a cottage; it consisted but of two rooms, if we may call them so, for really the upper apartment, which was the next storey to the ground floor, was next to the thatch, in which place he had often the benefit of contemplation; for though he was a smart large boy, his grandmother and he laid together, and between whiles the good old woman instructed Jack in many things, and among the rest: 'Jack,' says she, 'as you are a comfortable bedfellow to me, I must tell you I have a bean in my house which will make your fortune; you shall be richer than an emperor, you

* Deliberately tatty-looking beggar, designed to inspire pity.

47

shall have the whole world at your command; and as you now grow strong and lusty, I design to give it thee one day or other.'

'Oh,' says Jack, 'dear grandmother, give me now that bean, that I may try how rich I can be, and then how much I can love my dear grandmother.'

'No, child,' says she, 'should I do that, you would grow rich and turn rake, and you would never think of your poor grandmother again. But sirrah,' says she, 'if I was to know you would play such tricks, I would whip your little narley parley for you.'

'Nay,' says Jack, 'Grandmother, don't hurt me.'

'No,' answers the grandmother, 'you lusty boy, you know I love you too well to hit you. I love you as becomes me, and you ought to take notice of it.'

And so Jack made no words about the matter.

In the morning as Jack was making his grandmother's fire, pussycat scratching among the ashes clawed out the enchanted bean, which his grandmother had dropped out of her purse by accident. 'Odds budd,' says Jack, 'I'll set it in our garden, and see what it will come to, for I always loved beans and bacon.'

And then what was wonderful! The bean was no sooner put into the ground, but the sprout of it jumped out of the earth, and grew so quick that it gave Jack a fillip on the nose, and made him bleed furiously. In he runs to his grandmother, crying out, 'Dear grandmother, save me, I am killed.'

'No,' says she, 'I now have only time to tell you my enchantment will be broke in an hour's time, I know it, you have got me bean, and this impertinence of yours will occasion my being transformed; yet if I am able I will sufficiently thrash your jacket.'

But away runs Jack, and up the bean he climbs, and the old woman after him, with the birch broom in her hands. The bean was then about a mile high and by that time she got at it, Jack was straddled up near half a mile; and through her vengeance and ill-nature, not being able to reach the boy, she fell down in a fit for a time, and as soon as her hour was out, was turned into a monstrous toad and crawled into some neighbouring mud or cellar, on her way to the shades. But Jack went on his gallop, though the bean grew forty miles high, and while it was growing, some little towns were built upon the leaves as he went up, for him to refresh himself at. He called at one for a pot of ale, at another for bread and cheese, and at another, which was near the giant's castle, for what he could get; this had a very promising aspect, for the sign was as big as any on Ludgate Hill. Here he thought to rest for a time, and goes in strutting like a crow in a gutter.

'What have you to eat landlord?' says he.

'Everything in the world, sir,' says the landlord.

'Why then,' says Jack, 'give me a neck of mutton and broth.'

'Alas,' says the landlord, 'tomorrow is market day, how unfortunate it is! I cannot get you a neck of mutton tonight if I was to have my soul.'

'Well then get me something else,' says Jack. 'Have you any veal?'

'No, indeed, sir, not at present; but there is a fine calf fatting at Mr Jenkinson's, that will be killed on Saturday next.'

'But have you any beef in your house?' says Jack.

'Why truly, sir,' says the landlord, 'if you had been here on Monday last, I believe, though I say it should not say it, you never saw so fine a sirloin of beef as we had, and plum pudding too, which the justices who dined here, and their clerks and constables entirely demolished and though I got nothing by them, yet their company was a credit to my house.'

'Zounds,' says Jack, 'have you nothing in the house? I am hungry, I am starving; but I hear a cock crow, and from thence I am sure you have some poultry, kill one of them and broil it.'

'Yes sir,' says the landlord, 'but that cock is the squire's, he would not take forty guineas for it.'

'Well then,' replied Jack, 'you may kill a hen or chicken.'

'O, lord, sir, I have no chickens,' answered the landlord, 'and the two hens that I have belong to the game cock, and they have incubated, as I may say, their eggs a fortnight; but I believe we shall have chickens a week hence.'

'Have you no eggs in the house?' says Jack.

'No sir, indeed,' answers the landlord, 'but nest eggs, which we make of chalk.'

'Why then,' says Jack, 'what the devil have you got?'

'Why to tell you the truth, sir, I don't know that there is anything in the house to eat; for the squire and his huntsmen called here this morning and devoured what we had, all our bacon, all our cheese and all our bread; but I could only have got you some of the trouts from the Miller's only a little time before you came in he sent all his fish up to Sir John's.'

'Why then, says Jack, 'I find I must go to bed supperless.'

'Aye Master,' answers the host.

'Then give me some drink, says Jack. 'That I can do, for I have just brewed; and if you love new drink, I can fit you to a tittle, for it has not been in the tun half an hour.'

Thus was poor Jack plagued by the enchantment of his grandmother, who was resolved to lay him under her ill tongue, so long as her power lasted. But just as he fell in with this starving prospect, off goes the top of the house, the host was turned unto a beautiful lady; and in pops a dozen pretty youths, dressed like pages in green satin, laced with silver, and white feathers in their caps, each of them mounted upon a hobby-horse, finely bedecked with ribbons, tinsel and feathers; and in full chorus more harmoniously addressed themselves to Jack, saluting him with titles of Sovereign Lord of the Manor, and invincible champion. "Tis this instant that your supposed grandmother the Queen of Pomonkey has taken her passage to the shades, her enchantment is broke, and we bring you the full power of possessing all the pleasures you desire. The fair lady that stands before you is Empress of the Mountains of Moon: young as she seems to be, was your grandmother's black cat, and by enchantment has worn that shape four hundred years. It was she that put it in your mind to plant this wonderful bean by scratching in the ashes, and she is now entirely at your highness's disposal whether she shall live or die. You have a thousand Jack Catches now attending you without, with halters and hatchets to make an end of her, when your honour pleases to direct her execution; or else you have a fiery dragon gaping for her, if you give but the signal for her death. This box, great Sir, bears you the absolute power over her, over us, over old scratch, or Nicholas the Antient. Your grandmother, illustrious sir, when she found the loss of her bean, and the shortness of her power, invoked an assembly of inquietudes to attend you, and so transformed this miracle of nature into the host you have been talking with.'

'Why in troth,' says Jack, 'I thought it was a woman by filling me so full of expectation. But gentlemen, have you got any bread and cheese in your pockets, for I am bloody hungry? But since it is all enchantment, as I begin now to find by the alteration of my body, I feel sprinklings of generosity flow in my veins for my grandmother's dear pussycat, who has so often purred about me; I have nobleness of spirit to excuse my innocent landlord, and gratitude enough to take the fair lady to my arms.'

'It requires no more then, exalted monarch,' says the pages, 'but to put on the ring enclosed in that box, and you will instantly possess five wishes, and on the top of the ring your highness will find a marble red stone, given to your grandmother by the king of Strombolo. If you are engaged in combat, turn the stone to the north, and you may conquer giants, dragons and basilisks; and while you keep it to the south, you will flow in plenty and enjoy everything else you desire.'

'Is that all you have to say?' says Jack.

'Yes, and please your honour,' replied the pages.

And then Jack put on the ring; at which moment the remaining part of the inn was changed with a terrible crack into a delightful summer house or pavilion, where a table was spread with the most elegant dishes, and the sideboard furnished with the richest wines.

'This,' says Jack, 'pleases me above all things in the world, it is my first wish completely.' But then he espied his lady to be stark naked: 'I wish, Madam,' says Jack, 'you were as well clothed as the greatest queen in the world'; when immediately she was adorned with the gayest princely robes. 'Now,' says Jack, 'I wish for some good music'; and in an instant down came a dozen or two of excellent fiddles. He then wishes them to play the Black-Joke*, and so they went on for an hour, till he had crammed his carcass. And for the fifth he wished to be in bed with his fine lady; and as the laws of enchantment order it, a wish is no sooner thought on but executed, so were our couple enchanted into a crimson velvet bed, embroidered with

* Bawdy song popular around 1730, referenced in William Hogarth's 'A Rake's Progress'.

gold and pearls; the room illuminated with a hundred wax perfumed lights placed in glass sconces; the orange flowers, and the smaller ones made of mahogany and other fine wood, adorned with pyramids of sweetmeats and refreshing drams, from the true Barbados citron to humble. Neither was there wanting a chamber pot on each side of the bed, and a brace of closestools in separate closets, for fear of the worse; by which convenience lay the works of several eminent modern authors, by way of wipe. I should have observed that when the Princess was conjured into the wonderful apartments, she was attended by twelve damsels clothed in silver tissue who flew to her assistance mounted upon as many rosebuds. These were followed by an impudent shoe-boy, whose business it was to clean her ladyship's shoes against the morning. So that there was nothing wanting to complete the happiness of the illustrious couple. In short the attendants withdrew, and we leave them to play their rantum scantum tricks till the next morning. I may add that Jack had so much business upon his hands that night, that he fell asleep in the morning, and dreamt a dream in which the patroness of the enchantment appeared to him; and after having touched him and his princess three times with a wand, struck out of their memories all thoughts of what they had been and confirmed them in princely graces. Then whisking her wand three times over her head, whispered Prince John of his progress to the top of his bean, and how he should come to the castle of Giant Gogmagog, by whom himself and the Princess should be favourably received and entertained three days without danger, but he must be sure to keep the stone in his ring inclining to the north, and his princess on his north side, that then he should be in seeming danger of his life as well as his princess; but by turning the stone of his ring under the bent of his finger, the Princess would immediately change into a basilisk and kill all that were within reach of her eyes except himself; and then as soon as he could assure himself of safety, it was only to turn up his ring as it had been before, and then the Princess would resume her shape, and he become master of the giant's treasure. In the meantime she placed an enchanted fly upon the Princess's left breast to convey her as a flying horse would so, when she happened to be weary with climbing, and so departed.

Then Prince John began to rub his eyes, and stretching himself with a yawn or two, turned to his dear Princess who just waked from the same dream he himself had; there was the fly upon the breast of the lady, which they carefully took off and put into a little goblet which they found placed on a table by them, and after a merry turn or two, they disposed themselves for getting up, and were immediately attended with pages and virgins. They had a delightful breakfast, were dressed sumptuously, and set out for a walk towards the castle, the pages leading their hobby-horses in their hands, with one of an extraordinary kind and workmanship; for the Prince and the virgins had each hold of their rosebuds; and as for the Princess's enchanted fly, she had hung it in its cage, to the chain of her watch. It happened that the company by means of the enchanted air had got appetites like horses, and by agreement the Prince and Princess sat down under the side of a hill covered with orange trees and myrtles, the banks adorned with cowslips, primroses, Hyacinths, and violets; before them was a purling stream, and the words resounded with the harmonious notes of nightingales, linnets, canaries and other singing birds, when on a gentle breeze was seated an hundred cupids, each bearing a salver of gold garnished with the richest most delicate meats; when on the other hand, the trout, salmon, carp and other inhabitants of the stream, leaped upon the banks; with a proper supply of nectar, ambrosia, burgundy, champagne, hermitage, frontigniac and tokay wines, not forgetting a dram or two for the virgins of honour.

The Prince and Princess were delightfully regaled, whilst the zephyrs attended them with refreshing air; and when their company had satisfied themselves, the remainder of the entertainment vanished. And as it is not proper to walk much after a hearty repast, the Prince judged it convenient to ride the rest of the way towards the castle.

And now no sooner was the fly let out of its cage, but itself and all the hobby-horses and rosebuds were changed into palfreys, adorned with the richest trappings, and away they go in the grandest manner, passing by many knights and ladies, and were informed that there were many before them; when, on a sudden they heard a voice cry out (for they could hear many miles further than anyone else),

Fee-Faw-Fam
I smell the blood of an Englishman;
Whether he be alive or dead,
I'll grind his bones to make my bread.

But this did not trouble either the Prince or his lady or attendants; they all knew they had safety enough in their hands, and galloped on till they had arrived at the Castle of Wonders, when they soon espied the Giant Gogmagog, who was picking his teeth with a great tree: his toothpick case was such another thing as the Monument in London; he had a bowl of punch as big as St Paul's Church, and the cup that he drank out of was about the size of the Dome of St Paul's; for his tobacco pipe he had the exact model of the pyramidical building near the waterside at Southwark, where the damaged tobacco is burnt; and his tobacco stopper was like the water engine belonging to the York Building Company; and his tobacco box was about the size of Westminster Hall. But, however, he rose up when the Prince and his retinue appeared, and saluted them, bid them welcome, and offered them the best entertainment he could give them, but the Prince, for safety's sake, turned the stone of his ring to the north; for he had never seen so huge a man before.

They were introduced into the castle through the richest apartments imaginable; and what was extraordinary, the great giant shrunk into a common size, and appeared like other men. The furniture was vastly rich, the attendants without number, and the equipage magnificent and nothing was wanting to entertain our illustrious couple with splendour befitting their rank. The gardens were splendid as those at Versailles, the parks of vast extent, and, in a word, so well furnished with all sorts of game, that no other could parallel them, which pleased the young couple extremely, knowing full well they would be soon at their own disposal.

But they had now passed near the three days with the giant, who grew desperately in love with the Princess and resolved to have her at any rate, even at the expense of devouring her husband; which he could have done at a mouthful well enough, if he had been a common man. But enchantment is a great help to men in such distress, and the Prince and his lady went to bed well satisfied. They were no sooner laid down on their pillow, but they heard a mighty sobbing and mourning of many virgins, sighing and grieving at their hard fortunes, that the giant was to make a breakfast of them the next morning.

Now you must know, the stone in the Prince's ring being turned to the south, he could see and know what he pleased;

and having consulted with the Princess about the destruction of the giant: 'My dear,' says he, 'shall I make the proof of changing you into a cockatrice or basilisk, for there is a mouse in the room, and if your looks kill that animal we shall be sure of the rest, for it may be *multum in parvo**. The experiment was made in an instant, and the Princess's eyes and whole body became so bright, that it was even dazzling to her husband; and the mouse no sooner beheld her, but burnt with a prodigious crack. Then the ring was turned again, and all wishes were in the Prince's power; he immediately slipped through the keyholes of doors and narrow crannies, till he came to a large gallery, where several thousand ladies were tied up like calves o'fatting, and bemoaning their hard case. 'Alas! Dear Prince,' says they, 'tomorrow early shall we be broiled and crushed between the Giant Gogmagog's monstrous teeth, if you do not save us; and there are ten thousand knights below in as bad a condition.' 'You are then all safe,' says the Prince, 'for the giant will be destroyed as soon as the sun rises, and I shall then take possession of my dominions.

He had no sooner said this, but he released the ladies from their bridles, and summoned the Princess's virgins to attend to them with such necessaries as they wanted. Then he whisked through the cracks and keyholes, till he reached the place where the knights were confined; and they like the ladies were tied up to their good behaviour, and were moreover restrained the use of their hands, which he soon changed to their satisfaction, and gave them the assistance of his pages, with the promise to release them the next morning. Then were the rooms, where the prisoners of both sexes were

* Literally 'much in little', presumably here indicating that this experiment will serve as an illustration of the greater feat of giant-killing that is to follow.

kept, illuminated and furnished with every refreshing liquor; while the Prince returned to his Lady and related what had passed.

The day no sooner broke, but up got the Prince and Princess and walking into a bower refreshed themselves with some fruits, and the giant appeared with a sword in his hand, says he with a hoarse voice: 'Thou Prince of Pity, this moment you die, and the next instant will I solace myself in the delights of thy princess.' The Prince and Princess immediately got from their seats, and while the Prince was turning the ring towards the north, the giant hit him a thundering stroke with his sword; but he might as well have hit a rock of diamond as wound the Prince; for by this time the ring was in a proper station, and the Princess was changed into a cockatrice or basilisk. The giant at this gave a great groan, fell on his knees, trembled and fell down dead. Then there was a great shout in the castle, the doors flew open, the knights and ladies sallied forth to congratulate their highnesses; and proclaim them as their sovereigns; they became their vassals, and attended them in their delightful palace and royalty in the most perfect happiness.

And so far for enchantment, which some old women first set on foot to amuse children, and is not finished by the author, with no other view but to assure his readers, that enchantment proceeds from nothing but the chit chat of an old nurse, or the maggots in a madman's brain.

# BEAUTY AND THE BEAST

From *La Belle et la bête*, by Madame de Villeneuve, first published in 1740, abridged and translated by David Carter.

*The original work was in two parts. For this abridgement one continuous text has been produced. The last part of the story, after the Beast's retransformation, and which deals with the background story of Beauty's real father, has been the most extensively abridged.*

In a country very far away from here there was a large town, which counted among its citizens a merchant who was lucky in his enterprises and whom fortune had always showered with its finest favours. His family consisted of six boys and six daughters, none of whom had yet set up a home of their own. The boys were too young to be in much of a hurry, and the girls too proud to make up their minds quickly. But an unexpected reversal in the Merchant's fortunes upset their pleasant life. Their house caught fire destroying all the Merchant's goods except for a very few things. This disaster was but the first of many. The father lost all of his ships at the same time, either by their being sunk or attacked by corsairs, and his business partners let him down. Thus he fell suddenly into a state of terrible poverty.

The only thing left for him to do was to live with his family in a remote country place, more than a hundred leagues from the town. His daughters contemplated the prospect with horror. For a long time they had believed that they would be able to choose any husband they wanted. But when their father lost all his fortune their attentive crowd of admirers disappeared. So they found themselves isolated in a house in the middle of a forest. And as they could not afford to pay for any servants, the daughters had to do all the domestic chores.

Only the youngest of the daughters proved herself to be more steadfast and resolute. She also tried to cheer everyone up by playing music and singing, but her sisters were inconsolable, and regarded her efforts as petty.

This youngest daughter was also extremely beautiful, with a generous heart, and she came to be known by the name Beauty. She did everything she could to alleviate her father's sufferings.

Two years had passed and the family had started to get used to their rural life, when news came that one of the merchant's ships that he believed to be lost had returned loaded with goods. On hearing the news his daughters wanted to abandon everything and set off at once, but he persuaded them to stay and take care of the harvest, while he undertook the long journey himself.

All the daughters, except for the youngest, were now in no doubt that they would at least be able to live a comfortable life again in another town. Living in the country had not deprived them of their taste for luxury and they made their father promise to buy for them jewellery, necklaces and hairpieces. Noticing Beauty's silence the father asked her if there was something she wanted. She replied that she wanted something more precious than all the things her sisters had asked for, and that was the happiness of seeing him return safely. He insisted however that she ask for something else. Finally she agreed and asked him to bring her back a rose, which she had not been able to enjoy in their isolated situation.

And so he set off for the city, but his hopes were not to be fulfilled. The ship had arrived, but his associates thought he was dead and had disposed of the goods. Finally he had to set off for home again, but at a time when the weather was so bad, that he almost died of fatigue during the journey.

It took him several hours to get through the forest, and as everything was now covered in snow it was difficult to find his way. By chance he found himself at an avenue leading to a fine mansion. It seemed that the snow had left the avenue untouched. There were four lines of very high orange trees, loaded with both flowers and fruit, and many statues in various poses and placed in no particular arrangement, some on the pathway and others among the trees. Arriving in a courtyard he saw many other statues too. A staircase made of agate with a rail of chased gold presented itself to his view.

He went inside the mansion and passed through several magnificently furnished rooms. By now he was feeling hungry, but there was no one for him to turn to except statues. All the rooms were open, but there was no living being to be seen. After a while he stopped in one room where a huge fire had been lit and he sat down next to it. Soon he was overcome by tiredness. When he woke up he was agreeably surprised to find a table full of inviting delicacies. After eating he wanted to thank his hosts, but the food had made him tired again and he fell asleep again for at least four hours. On waking again he found another table of porphyry with a selection of cakes, dried fruits and liqueur wines.

Still no person appeared in the mansion and he began to feel afraid. He began to think that, for reasons he could not fathom, some kind of Intelligent Being was making him a gift of this house with all its riches. He started to imagine how he would distribute its treasures among his children. He went into the garden, where, despite the harshness of winter, he could see, as though it were the middle of spring, the rarest of flowers. Birdsong was blended with the sound of fountains in a pleasant harmony.

On his arrival at the mansion he had noticed a path lined with flowering rose trees. He had never seen such beautiful roses and their scent reminded him of his promise to Beauty. He picked one and was about to make six bouquets, when a terrible noise made him turn his head. He was terrified to see nearby a horrible beast, which touched him on the collar with a kind of trunk similar to that of an elephant, and said to him in a dreadful voice, 'Who gave you the right to pick my roses? Wasn't it enough that I treated you with so much kindness in my palace? Your insolence will not go unpunished.' The old man was terrified at the appearance of this monster and begged him to have pity on him. The monster was angered by the way the old man addressed him and said to him, 'I am the Beast, and you will not escape the death you deserve.' The old man tried to explain that the rose he had picked was for one of his daughters called Beauty. He told him about his problems, his journey and his daughters' requests.

The Beast thought for a moment and then continued in a less angry tone: 'I would like to pardon you but only on condition that you give me one of your daughters.' The old man asked the Beast how he could possibly make one of his daughters come there, to which the Beast replied that the daughter he brought would have to come voluntarily or not at all. 'Choose one of them who is willing to do it to save your life, and then return with her to me in one month's time. If you can't choose one then you must promise me, as a man of honour, that you will return alone. I warn you that if you agree just to get away from here, I will find you and destroy you and your family.' The old man finally agreed to the terms and the Beast told him to stay for one more night and enjoy his hospitality before departing on a horse which he would provide for him. The Beast also told him that he could take one rose for Beauty, and that the same horse which he would ride the next day would come for him and his daughter at the appointed time.

The next morning after taking breakfast the old man found the horse, and as soon as he had mounted it, it departed at an incredible speed. The horse took the old man at an unimaginable speed back towards his home. When he considered turning the horse round and going back he found that it would not let him. As he neared his house he resolved not to tell his daughters about the threat to his life. When the daughters saw him arrive on a superb horse and in fine clothes they were at first full of joy, but then they became anxious on seeing the sadness on his face and the tears in his eyes.

He presented the rose to Beauty and hinted that it had cost him dear. This made his children inquisitive and made him give up his resolution not to tell them what had happened to him, both in pursuit of his lost fortune and at the monster's palace. His sons proposed that one of them should face the Beast's wrath. The older daughters argued that it was because Beauty had not asked for valuable things as they had, that the disaster had befallen them.

Beauty was happy to pay with her life for the sake of someone who had given her life. Her brothers recognised the firmness of her resolution and praised her for it.

Only the father would not at first agree, but Beauty insisted that she would do it even if he would not accept her sacrifice. She tried to reassure him that perhaps while her fate seemed dreadful some good might come of it. At this her sisters only smiled maliciously.

Finally the day arrived when the horse came to take her away. Her brothers wanted to slaughter the horse but she made them realise that it was pointless to attempt it. And so Beauty and her father mounted the horse which flew rather than galloped away.

On their journey the old man tried to persuade his daughter to give up her resolve, but she said that as she was now prepared for death, it did not matter whether her killer was attractive or hideous. And so they flew on, and as night came all kinds of marvellous lights appeared to guide their way. Finally they reached the avenue of orange trees, and all the lights suddenly disappeared to be replaced by torches held in the hands of the statues. The whole façade of the palace was covered with paper lanterns, and as they entered the courtyard salvoes were fired in charming harmony.

The horse stopped at a flight of steps, and the two dismounted. Her father led Beauty to the room where he had been so well treated. There they found a huge fire, scented candles and a splendid meal waiting for them.

Beauty began to think that perhaps her fate would not be as dreadful as she had expected. The horrible Beast that she had been threatened with did not reveal itself. Soon however it made itself heard. Its arrival was announced by a horrible noise caused by the enormous weight of its body, the terrible clattering sound of its scales and an awful howling. Beauty was seized with terror and her father put his arms round her. She soon braced herself however and greeted the Beast respectfully. This seemed to please the monster, who said 'Good evening, sir' to the father, and turning to Beauty said 'Good Evening, Beauty.'

The Beast asked her if she had come voluntarily and she assured him that she had. The Beast then told the old man that the horse would take him home the following day after breakfast, and that he should not attempt to return. He also told them both to select some gifts from the dressing room nearby which the father could take in two trunks for Beauty's brothers and sisters. When the Beast had left them they opened the cabinets in the room, one of which contained all kinds of precious stones and another gold coins. Beauty suggested to her father that it would be better for him to take some of the coins rather than jewellery, because he could use them without drawing attention to his wealth. The old man agreed but decided to take at least a few gifts for his daughters and said he would conceal his new-found wealth from everyone, even his children, who would otherwise want to leave their country home.

The next morning there were two horses waiting for the old man one was the same one which had brought them to the palace and the other was loaded with the two trunks. So as not to annoy the Beast the old man took his leave as quickly as possible, and Beauty went to the room she had been given full of tears. After such an exhausting month she was overcome by tiredness and finding some chocolate drink prepared for her on the bedside table she fell asleep. And as she slept she dreamt.

She dreamt that she was on the bank of a canal that stretched off to infinity, and both sides of which were decorated by orange trees and very tall flowering myrtles. A beautiful young man, like the figure of Amor itself, spoke to her: 'Don't think that you will be as unhappy as you fear. You can help me shake off my disguise. You must judge whether my company is despicable and is not to be preferred to that of a family that is not worthy of you. I love you and we can be perfectly happy together.'

After this first dream she seemed to be in a small but magnificent room with a woman whose majesty and surprising beauty inspired her with profound respect. The woman said to her, 'Beauty, do not regret the life you have left. A more illustrious fate awaits you, but you must not allow yourself to be seduced by appearances.' Then she dreamt of the young man in many different situations until she was woken up by the daylight.

A clock sounded her name a dozen times in musical tones, and so she got up from her bed, dressed herself and went into a room where a meal had been prepared for her. She could not forget the beautiful young man who had appeared in her dream, and thought that he must be kept a prisoner somewhere in the palace. Finally she realised that she had better turn her thoughts to her present fate, and set off to explore the numerous apartments of the palace.

The first room was full of mirrors and there was also a portrait of a handsome cavalier, just like the young man she had seen in her dream. She also found a bracelet which she put on her arm, not considering whether she should do so or not.

Next she passed through a gallery of paintings where she found a life-size portrait of the same man, who seemed to be looking at her tenderly.

Beauty then found herself in a room full of different kinds of instruments. She knew how to play almost all of them and tried out some of them, preferring the harpsichord above all, because it provided the best accompaniment to her voice. Then she went into another gallery which contained a huge library. She had always loved reading but her father had been forced to sell his library when they had to live in the country. And so the day passed by without her being able to see every part of the mansion.

At the usual hour Beauty found dinner served for her, without the appearance of a single human figure. Finally she heard the Beast approaching again and was full of foreboding at being alone with him for the first time. But his manner showed no signs of anger and he said simply 'Good evening, Beauty.' They talked only about how she had spent her day. After an hour or so she realised that he was more stupid than angry. Then he asked her directly if she would let him sleep with her. At such an unexpected request she could not help crying out 'Oh heavens, I am lost!'

'Not at all,' replied the Beast calmly. 'Simply answer yes or no.' Trembling she replied, 'No.' And the Beast said, 'As you do not wish it I shall leave you. Goodnight, Beauty.' Relieved, Beauty said 'Goodnight.' When she finally went to bed she dreamt again of the beloved stranger.

The young man said to her, 'How happy I am to see you again, Beauty. But it seems that I shall be unhappy for a long time.' He appeared to her in many different ways. At one moment he was presenting her with a crown, at another he was at her feet, now overwhelmed with joy, now in tears. When she woke up she hurried to the gallery of paintings to admire his portrait again. To distract her thoughts she went down into the gardens, as the weather was so fine.

She was surprised to discover many of the places where she had seen the stranger in her dreams, and became more convinced that the Beast was keeping him prisoner in his palace. She then wandered through the apartments which she had not seen the previous day, and they were just as interesting as the others. In one was an aviary full of rare birds, which approached her in a friendly way. She lamented to them that they were not nearer to her own room, so that she could hear them often. Then to her surprise she opened another door only to find herself back in her own room.

Continuing her walk she encountered some parrots of many different species and colours. Each of them talked to her about something different, some of them even sang arias from opera or proclaimed verses by the best authors. As she did not enjoy silence she chose one to accompany her, reassuring the others that they could visit her whenever they wanted.

Not far away she also discovered a large group of monkeys of all sizes and colours. They accompanied her back to her apartment. She invited some of them to keep her company. At that very moment two female monkeys dressed as ladies of the court appeared at her side with two small monkeys following them like pages. A Barbary ape dressed like a Spanish gentleman also went with them. And so Beauty went in to dinner, which was accompanied by the singing birds. The monkeys served her at table like courtiers.

After the meal she was treated to another spectacle. The monkeys dressed themselves up in theatrical costumes and performed a tragedy, with the parrots pronouncing the words. Beauty found it all enchanting.

Then the Beast arrived as usual and after the same questions and the same responses he finished with his usual, 'Goodnight, Beauty.'

The female monkeys then accompanied Beauty to her room, undressed her and put her to bed.

Several days passed in this fashion, and she put up with the brief nightly visits by the Beast, because she realised that it was he who made all these pleasures possible. Several times she was tempted to ask him about the young man who visited her in her dreams, but, although the monster seemed to be gentle enough, she was afraid of making him jealous.

On one occasion Beauty went into a large room which she had only seen once before. In this room there were four windows on each side. Only two were open, and outside it seemed to be dark, so Beauty tried to let in more light, but she found only a space covered by a veil through which she could see a distant glimmer of light. When she lifted the veil she discovered a theatre. She watched several performances. Then she noticed that her box was separated from the next one by a mirror and that everything that she thought had been real was in fact an illusion. The glass reflected the image of the most beautiful city in the world above the stage. After having watched all the fine people leaving the theatre she went down into the garden again.

After dinner the Beast came to her as usual to ask her how she had enjoyed her day, and she told him about her visit to the theatre. Finally he put his usual question, 'Would you like me to sleep with you?' She said no as usual and pondered over her situation for a long time, so that it was almost dawn before she went to bed. The stranger appeared to her immediately and reproached her gently for keeping him waiting. He wanted to know why she was so sad and she explained to him that the Beast clearly loved her but that he, the stranger, had made it impossible for any other to win her heart. He said, 'Love the one who loves you. Do not let yourself be deceived by appearances. And free me from my prison.' She saw all kinds of fantastic things: the monster sitting on a bright jewelled throne inviting her to sit beside him, and the stranger sitting there himself. The stranger disappeared and he was talking behind a black veil, which changed his voice and made it sound horrible.

Later that day Beauty watched a different performance. This time she was at the opera, which started as soon as she took her seat. The mirrors enabled her to see many of the people in the stalls, including some she knew.

The following day she opened a third window and found herself at the Saint-Germain fair. Here she saw all kinds of unusual things: extraordinary natural phenomena, works of art, a puppet show and the Opéra-Comique.

After these spectacles she enjoyed walking among the merchants' stalls and watching the professional gamblers. At times she wanted to intervene to warn some players that they were being deceived but she was in reality thousands of leagues away and could neither be seen nor heard by them.

It was after midnight before she thought of retiring. The Beast noticed her impatience. The following days were similar. The other three windows provided her with the pleasures of visiting the Italian Comedy, and seeing the Tuileries, where she could see all kinds of distinguished people. The last window enabled her to see what was happening in the whole world: sometimes she saw a famous ambassador, sometimes an illustrious marriage and sometimes some interesting revolutions.

When Beauty had become sure that the Beast's character was essentially gentle and that he would not go into a rage, she asked him if they were alone in the palace. He assured her that apart from himself, her and the animals, there was no other being there. That evening the Beast left more abruptly than usual. Now it seemed that the young man only existed in her own imagination, Beauty started to regard the palace as a prison which would become her tomb.

These sad thoughts also disturbed her night. She seemed to be on the bank of a large canal. The stranger came to her and was alarmed at her sadness. He told her he would do all in his power to relieve her suffering. Even if it were the very sight of the Beast that grieved her he would free her from his power. It seemed to Beauty that the stranger drew out a dagger and was about to cut the throat of the monster, who made no effort to defend himself. She exclaimed, 'Stop, leave my benefactor alone. Rather you should kill me. I owe everything to the

Beast. He anticipates all my desires. It was through him that I got to know you, and I would rather die than that you should offend him in the least.'

After some time the figures disappeared and Beauty saw the lady she had seen several nights before, who told her to take courage and promised her that she would be happy if she did not rely on deceptive appearances.

During the day after she had this dream Beauty started to feel the need to see her father again. She became restless both at night and during the day, and for many days she could not settle down to enjoy the spectacles presented for her in any of the six windows.

It was difficult to conceal her sorrow from the Beast, but one evening she finally revealed to him that she wanted to see her family again. The Beast uttered a sigh and cried, 'What! You prefer a life with your jealous sisters, to all the delights available to you here? I think you want to leave out of hatred for me.'

Beauty contradicted him and requested that he allow her to return to her family for just two months, promising to come back and spend the rest of her life with him.

The Beast replied, 'I cannot refuse you anything but it may well cost me my life.' And he told her to fill four boxes with whatever gifts she wanted to take and return to her family for two months. At the end of that time she would need no horse and carriage, but would just have to lie in bed and twist the ring on her finger while she uttered the words, 'I want to return to my palace and see my Beast again.'

When she slept that night she saw the stranger again but he seemed to be overcome by profound grief. She asked him the cause and he could only say that it was because of her departure. She explained to him her reasons for going and that she would return again soon. He doubted that she would return just to save the life of a monster.

Almost angrily Beauty exclaimed, 'He is only a monster in appearance but human at heart. I could not repay his generosity with such ingratitude.'

After this dream she slept for a long time, and when she awoke she was surprised to hear a human voice that she recognised. Drawing the curtains she found herself in a room she did not recognise with furniture which was not so splendid as that in the Beast's palace. Somehow she had been transported together with the four boxes she had packed the previous night to a strange place. Then hearing the voice of her father she realised that she was at home with her family. Everyone looked at her as though she had just arrived from another world, and her sisters seemed to be as jealous of her as ever.

Her father had however regained some trust in the Beast's intentions. He told her how he had used wisely the wealth vouchsafed him by the Beast. He now looked forward to having her live with them again, but Beauty explained to him her situation and that she must return to the Beast in two months. Finally he advised her to marry the Beast as there was such a fine soul in that ugly body. It was far better, he said, to marry a man for his lovable qualities than for his handsome appearance.

Beauty agreed with him but still found it difficult to contemplate marrying such a horrible monster, especially as conversation with him was not at all interesting. She told him of the limits of their nightly talks, ending with the phrase, 'Goodnight, Beauty,' which the parrots could now say by heart. She would rather suffer a sudden death than die every day from fear, grief, disgust and boredom.

Her father understood his daughter's attitude but believed that the evidence of so much kindness and the good taste displayed in his palace showed that the Beast could not be so stupid. He also reminded her of the advice that the lady had given her in her dreams.

Despite her father's arguments Beauty could not be persuaded. That night she went to bed in expectation of seeing her beloved stranger again, but although she conjured up the places where they used to meet together, he did not appear, and it was a long boring night for her.

Beauty's father had used some of his wealth to buy a house in a large town. When it was heard that his youngest daughter had returned, everyone wanted to see her. She appeared more beautiful and more charming than ever, and her sisters' admirers found themselves attracted to her, much to the annoyance of the sisters, who began to hate her even more. All this determined Beauty to leave her family earlier than she intended. However she found it difficult to take leave of her family and kept deferring her departure, even when the two months had passed. Then she had a dream which caused her to make up her mind.

She dreamt that she was on a broad path near the Beast's palace. At the end of the path a thick wooded area covered the entrance to a cave, from where the most dreadful moaning sounds were coming. She recognised the Beast's voice and ran to his aid. She found him lying down and obviously dying. He blamed her for his sorry state. Then she saw the lady again who warned her that if she did not keep her promise and return immediately the Beast would die. Then Beauty awoke suddenly and afraid of causing the Beast's death she told her family that she would leave them. Everyone tried to dissuade her, except her sisters, who tried to cover up their jealousy with protestations of support. Despite all attempts to stop her therefore, Beauty retired to bed, explaining to her family that she would be gone before they awoke the next morning. Then, before getting into bed, she twisted the ring on her finger.

She slept long, and was awakened by the sound of the clock sounding her name twelve times in musical tones. By this she knew that her wishes had been fulfilled. The first day of her return seemed long, because she was impatient to see the Beast again and also, in her sleep, the stranger, whose company she had been deprived of for two months. She tried to distract herself by watching the Comédie-Française and the opera but everything bored her, even the animals. Finally the hour arrived at which the Beast usually appeared, but there was no sign of him. She ran out into the gardens, determined to find him. Finally after three hours she sat down on a bench and felt that she must be alone in the palace. It seemed extraordinary to her that she had such strong feelings for the monster.

Sobbing to herself she realised that she was on the very path where she had been in her dream the night before she left her father's house. She saw a hollow lair which looked like that she had seen in her dream. With monkeys to light her way with torches she found the Beast lying down on the earth. She caressed his head, but finding his body cold she was certain that he was dead. Putting her hand on his heart however, she sensed that he was still breathing.

With the help of the monkeys she brought some water from a nearby fountain, to refresh him. Eventually he regained consciousness. She said to the Beast, 'I did not know how much I loved you. The fear of losing you made me realise that I was joined to you by bonds stronger than gratitude. I could only think of dying if I had not been able to save your life.' The Beast was relieved at hearing these words and replied, 'I also

74

love you more than my own life. If I thought I would never see you again I would die. Go to bed and you can be certain that you will be happy in the way that your good heart deserves.' Beauty now no longer considered him to be stupid, but found in his short replies a sign of wisdom.

Very exhausted, Beauty quickly fell asleep and soon her beloved stranger appeared. He promised her that she would be happy, and when she asked if this would mean marrying the Beast, he replied that it was the only way. Then she dreamt that the Beast was lying dead at her feet, and immediately after this the stranger appeared and then immediately disappeared, his place being taken by the Beast. She then saw the lady very clearly, who told her not to worry and that she would ensure her happiness. She would find perfect happiness if she married the Beast.

Throughout the following day she remained uncertain about what to do, and felt that only the arrival of the Beast would help her to decide. He did not reproach her for her long absence but only expressed concern for her welfare, and then as usual before taking his leave he asked her if she wanted to sleep with him. She took some time to reply but finally said, 'Yes, I will, provided that you make a vow to me.' And he agreed, vowing never to have another spouse, while she promised to love him faithfully and with affection.

Scarcely had she spoken when artillery fire was heard and for three hours the sky was illuminated by thousands of rockets. Finally the Beast suggested that it was time to go to bed. She was pleasantly surprised that when the lights went out and her husband lay down beside her he did so very lightly and was soon asleep. She also soon fell asleep and her beloved stranger came to her immediately, and told her that she had freed him from his terrible imprisonment: 'Your marriage with the Beast will return a king to his subjects, a son to his mother and life to his kingdom. Everyone will be happy.' This did not however reassure Beauty. Then the lady appeared and told her that no one else would ever enjoy happiness of the kind that her virtue had brought her. Then she saw the young man again, but lying down as though he were dead.

When she awoke in the morning she thought that she was still dreaming. But it was undoubtedly real. Instead of the Beast she found her beloved stranger. And he looked a thousand times more handsome than he had during the night. Despite her best efforts however she could not wake him. He seemed to be under some kind of spell. As he was indeed her husband she allowed herself the liberty of kissing him a thousand times, in the hope of waking him up. It made her so happy to think that she had done out of duty what she had wanted to do out of preference. But still her husband did not wake up.

Then she heard the sound of a carriage arriving below the windows of her apartment and voices of people approaching her room. Looking out of the window she saw a magnificent carriage pulled by four white stags with golden antlers. She went into the anteroom and met there two ladies, one of them being the one who had appeared to her in her dreams and the other was just as beautiful and clearly an illustrious person. The lady already known to her turned to the other and said, 'Well, Your Majesty, what do you think of this beautiful girl, to whom you owe your son's return to life? The prince would have remained transformed into that horrible form, if it had not been possible to find one person in the world whose virtue and courage were equal to her beauty. Their perfect happiness lacks but your consent.'

At these words the Queen embraced Beauty and congratulated her, asking her also who were the parents of such a perfect princess. When Beauty described her origins to her she was obviously shocked: 'What, you are only the daughter of a merchant!' She looked at the other lady in dismay, and cried, 'Oh, Madam Fairy!'

The other lady, who was indeed a Grand Fairy, informed her that she was the only suitable girl that could be found in the whole world. The Queen replied that she was sure it was not impossible to find a girl whose virtue was equal to her high birth.

At that moment the handsome stranger appeared, awoken by the arrival of his mother and the Grand Fairy. The noisy dispute had proved more powerful than all Beauty's efforts to wake him. The Queen embraced him in silence for a long time. The Prince himself was so happy to find himself free from his dreadful appearance and from the distressing stupidity imposed on him, which had fortunately not obscured his reason. He gave thanks also to the Grand Fairy. What he felt for Beauty he had already indicated by the way he looked at her. The Grand Fairy reminded him that he should decide between his mother's judgement and hers regarding Beauty. She asked Beauty, 'Would you want a husband who had any regrets about his choice?'

'Certainly not, Madam,' replied Beauty, 'I renounce the honour of being his wife. I became engaged to him to do him a great favour.'

'What do you think, Your Majesty?' said the Grand Fairy scornfully. 'Don't you think that her virtue lends her a sufficiently high status?'

The Queen replied that of course Beauty was an incomparable person, but wondered if they could not find other means to reward her than by sacrificing her son's hand.

Beauty said to the Queen that she required no other reward than to be with her father again.

The Prince was unable to contain himself any longer and threw himself at his mother's feet to beg her not to deprive him of the joy of being her husband.

Beauty tried to console him by saying that as she had renounced his love for the sake of the Beast, so she could renounce him for his own sake.

The Prince then begged the Grand Fairy to make him into a monster again so that she might continue to love him. The Grand Fairy did not reply but watched the Queen who was obviously touched by the scene, though her pride was not weakened.

For several minutes nobody spoke a word, until the Grand Fairy eventually broke the silence: 'I think you both deserve each other and I promise that you can stay together. I have the power to ensure it.' She also pointed out that the Prince would never be able to regret the marriage on grounds of inequality. She turned to the Queen and said proudly, 'She is your niece! And she is made respectable by the fact that she is also mine, as she is the daughter of my sister. She married the King of the Happy Isle, your brother. Since she was born I have so arranged her destiny that she should become the wife of your son.'

The Queen was confused, but she embraced Beauty and told her that her reluctance had only been due to the fact that she wished to have her son marry the niece that the Grand Fairy had assured her was still alive.

The Grand Fairy said that only one thing was missing to complete these happy circumstances and that was the consent of the King, Beauty's true father, but he would soon arrive. Beauty begged her also to allow the old man whom she had regarded as her father to be present, and the Grand Fairy agreed to arrange it.

The Grand Fairy led the Queen away under the pretext of showing her the enchanted palace, in order to allow the newlyweds to spend some time together for the first time.

The confused conversation that took place between the couple was more certain proof of their love than eloquence could have been. And Beauty was at last able to ask the Prince how it had come about that he had been transformed so cruelly. The Prince finished his account and Beauty was about to say something to him when she was prevented by the loud sound of voices and rattling weapons. Everyone looked out of the windows and saw a troop of soldiers and courtiers dressed for hunting. The man at the head had all the appearances of a king. At this sight the Grand Fairy turned to the Queen and said, 'It's the King, your brother, and Beauty's father. He will be delighted, for, as you know, he has long believed his daughter to be dead.'

As the King dismounted Beauty rushed towards him, threw herself down before him, embraced his legs and addressed him as her father. The King was obviously confused. Then he recognised his sister, the Queen, who also embraced him and presented her son to him. She explained to him the debt they owed to Beauty and recounted details of all that had happened.

The Grand Fairy asked him if the young woman did not remind him of someone he knew, and he hardly dared admit that she resembled the daughter who, according to certain evidence, had been devoured by wild animals. On reflection he did think that she was like his wife who had died. The

Grand Fairy assured him that she was indeed his daughter, and invited him into the palace, so that she could tell him the rest of the story. And as they went into the palace the Grand Fairy used her powers to bring back to life all the statues. And when everybody was in the palace the Grand Fairy began to relate full details of what had happened in the past, addressing herself to the King.

She explained for everyone's sake the laws of the Happy Isle, by which all the inhabitants were allowed to marry whomsoever they wished. Thus the King himself had chosen to marry a young shepherdess. Unknown to the King she was a fairy and also the Grand Fairy's sister. The fairy laws forbid marriage to anyone who does not have the same powers as they do, and her sister attempted to keep her marriage secret.

When the fairies found out, the King's wife was deprived of her status and condemned to imprisonment. Some of the fairies took pity on her, but one decrepit old fairy demanded that she be punished by having her daughter marry a monster. Unfortunately the majority of the fairies supported this decision.

When the King's wife was condemned to imprisonment it was decided to persuade the King that she had died. The fairy who had first revealed the secret now kidnapped another queen and took on her appearance. In this form she threw herself at the King's feet imploring him to help her. She feigned a liking for his daughter and asked him to let her be in charge of her education. Eventually she also attempted to persuade him to marry her but the King did not want a stepmother for his daughter and was only willing to play the role of supportive neighbour.

The evil fairy developed a hatred for Beauty as strong as that for her mother, and began to realise that the only way to win any influence over the King was to have his daughter killed. She arranged for the girl's governess and her husband to kill the child in a nearby forest where there would be no witnesses and to explain that she had died suddenly. Now the Grand Fairy had agreed to watch over the fate of her sister's child and when she learned of the plan she took on the form of a monstrous bear and hid in the forest where the murder was to happen. She strangled the governess and her companion and left signs to indicate that the child had been killed too, but in fact took her away with her.

She found a small house where a peasant family which appeared to be fairly well off was living. The family was asleep and a sick child lay beside them. The Grand fairy attempted to bring it back to health but it died as she touched it. As it was a girl she decided to replace it with the live child she was carrying. She buried the dead child and returned to the house.

She learned from the peasants that the child was that of a rich merchant and one of them was its wet nurse. They had brought it to the countryside because it was ill and they thought the country air would do it good. Seeing that this had been successful they decided to take it back to its father.

The Grand Fairy was still concerned about how she could find some way of saving Beauty from her fate of marrying a monster. When she learned how the young prince had been changed into a monster she realised that this was the opportunity she had been seeking to turn Beauty's fate to good advantage. Thus she arranged for them to fall in love with each other, and she brought everything to a happy conclusion.

Then suddenly they were all surprised by a symphony of beautiful sounds which announced the arrival of a charming troop of fairies, and amongst them was the Grand Fairy's sister and wife of the King. Amazed and delighted the King embraced her. She explained how she had agreed to do a special favour for the Queen of the Fairies and had been granted her freedom as a result.

Beauty did not forget the old merchant and reminded the Grand Fairy of her promise. She had barely finished speaking before they heard the sound of horses arriving in the courtyard. They had brought with them her entire family: the old Merchant, his sons, daughters and their lovers. All looked confused at their sudden arrival at the palace. The Grand Fairy reminded the merchant that he should forsake the role of father and that he should now pay homage to Beauty as his sovereign. She identified all the illustrious persons present to him. Beauty persuaded the Prince and the others to let her retain the titles of father, brothers and sisters for the family which had brought her up. And all were given positions of rank in Beauty's court.

The wedding festivities of Beauty and the Prince lasted several days. The Grand Fairy finally had to remind the couple that it was time to return to their kingdom and present themselves to their subjects. They agreed but made her promise to let them return to this place occasionally to relive their magical experiences. And so the Grand Fairy provided them with a carriage pulled by a dozen white stags with gold-tipped horns to take them off to their kingdom.

And the Queen, the Prince's mother, did not fail to record this marvellous story in the archives of the empire and in those of the Happy Isle, to pass it on to posterity. Thus for all eternity people have talked of the wonderful adventures of Beauty and the Beast.

## THE LITTLE MERMAID

From *Undine* by Friedrich de la Motte Fouqué, first published
in 1811, abridged and translated by David Carter.

*Fouqué divided his story into nineteen chapters, each of which
was developed with great skill, creating suspense and expectation of what might come in the next chapter. Each chapter was
also provided with a heading which heightened the interest.
In this abridgement some sense of the structure of the original
has been maintained by leaving several lines blank where the
chapter divisions originally were.*

*Many of the names of characters have specific associations in
German, such as 'Kühleborn'('Cool Spring') and 'Heilmann'
('Holy or Healing Man'), etc., but the translator feels that
nothing would be gained by translating them literally.*

*It is to be hoped that a reading of this abridgement will
encourage the reader to seek out a copy of the complete work.*

It may well be already many hundreds of years ago now, that
a good old fisherman was once sitting in front of his door on
a beautiful evening mending his nets. He lived in a very charming area. The green earth on which his hut was built stretched
out far into a large lake. Very few if any human beings were to
be encountered in this pretty spot, except for the Fisherman
and those he lived with. For behind the spit of land lay a wild
forest of which most people were only too afraid, and would
not go into it if it were not necessary, because it was said
that one would encounter strange creatures and phantoms
there. The pious old Fisherman passed through it many times
without any trouble however, because he always harboured
only pious thoughts and sang religious songs.

On this particular evening he suddenly heard a rustling sound in the darkness of the forest like that of a man and his horse, and as he turned to look in that direction it seemed to him that he saw the giant figure of a man in white coming towards him, but pulling himself together he realised that it was just the foaming water of a familiar stream. The sound however was caused by a finely dressed knight on a white stallion who was coming out of the shade of the trees towards his hut. The Fisherman was only too pleased to welcome him as a guest and the Knight dismounted, saying that he had in any case no alternative as he did not wish to go back into the strange forest.

Inside the hut the Knight was welcomed by the Fisherman's old wife, who bade him sit down. The couple learned that their guest's name was Huldbrand von Ringstetten and enjoyed his account of his travels and of his castle near the source of the Danube. From time to time during their conversation they heard a sound as though someone were splashing water against the low window. Finally the old man stood up and shouted out in a threatening voice towards the window: 'Undine! Will you stop once and for all this childish behaviour? Especially as we have a stranger as guest in the hut tonight!' Outside it became quiet except for a slight giggling, and the old man explained that it was their foster daughter, Undine, who refused to put off her childish ways, although she was already about eighteen years old.

Then the door flew open and a beautiful blond-haired girl slipped in laughing, and said, 'You're teasing me, father. Where is your guest?' At the same moment she became aware of the Knight and stood in amazement at the beautiful young man. Huldbrand was likewise delighted at the charming creature. Then she came up close to him and, playing with the golden coin hanging on a valuable chain at his breast, asked him in flattering tones, how he came to be there. When Huldbrand said that he had come through the forest she demanded that he tell about his adventures there. But the old man said it was not a good time for such matters. At this Undine stamped her foot on the floor and insisted, but in such a charming way that Huldbrand found her only more attractive. The old couple scolded her for her ill-mannered behaviour, and Undine, unable to get her way, dashed out into the night.

Huldbrand and the Fisherman sprang up from their seats and wanted to go after the angry girl. 'We must call after her,' said Huldbrand, 'and ask her to come back.' And he called her name urgently many times. But the old man shook his head and said it would not help.

They finally went back inside the hut, where the old woman had already gone to bed, being used to Undine's behaviour. They sat down by the fire and the old man suggested they spend part of the night chatting over a jug of wine. He then told the Knight the story of how Undine had come to them.

'It was probably about fifteen years ago when I went off one day through the wild forest to take my wares to the town on the other side. My wife had stayed at home as usual, because God had blessed us, at quite an advanced age, with a really beautiful little girl. On my way back from the town and on this side of the forest my wife came towards me with eyes full of tears and in mourning. She told me how she had been playing with the child on the shore of the lake, and the child had leaned forward, as though she had seen something very beautiful in the water, and reaching out towards it, she had fallen out of my wife's arms and into the watery mirror before her.

'We spent the evening staring tearfully into the fire. Then we heard a rustling sound at the door. The door burst open and there on the threshold stood a beautiful little girl about three or four years old, smiling at us, and dressed in fine clothes. Then I noticed the water dripping from her clothes and realised that she had been lying in the water. I said to my wife that, as nobody had been able to rescue our own child for us, we should at least do for this child what we would have wanted others to do for us. So we looked after her and put her to bed.

'The next day we tried to find out where she had come from, but she has always told us only such strange things, about golden castles, crystal roofs and that she fell out of a boat into water and found herself under the trees.

'She insisted that her parents had called her Undine, which seemed to me to be a heathen name. I consulted a priest in the town, and although he did not like the idea at first he succumbed to her charms and agreed to baptise her Undine.'

Here the Knight interrupted the Fisherman to draw his attention to a noise like that of a powerfully rushing flood of water, which he had also noticed earlier during the old man's story. They rushed to the door and saw that the stream that came from the forest had burst its banks and was dragging stones and branches with it in a raging torrent. Shouting out Undine's name both men rushed out of the hut.

Huldbrand finally came to the edge of the stream and could see how it had now turned the spit of land into an island. He climbed across some stones and fallen trees trying to find Undine on the other side. He seemed to see the long white figure of a man grinning and nodding at him from the far bank. Then he heard a familiar voice warning him, 'Don't trust him, don't trust him! The old man, the stream, he's treacherous!' He caught sight of Undine lying down on the grass on a small island formed by the flood. With a few more steps he was by her side. By then the Fisherman had also reached the bank of the stream and called out to Huldbrand to bring her back onto firm land. Eventually she agreed as long as Huldbrand was allowed to tell her about his experiences in the forest. He carried her back across the stream where she was embraced by the old man. Finally all was forgiven and the old couple were reconciled with Undine.

As the storm faded away and the dawn light shone over the lake, they all sat having breakfast under the trees. With Undine sitting at his feet, Huldbrand began to tell his story.

'It must have been about eight days ago that I rode into the free imperial city which lies on the other side of the forest. There was soon to be a tournament including racing, which I took part in. While resting by the barrier on one occasion I caught sight of a beautiful woman on a balcony. I found out that the young virgin's name was Bertalda and that she was the foster daughter of a powerful duke who lived in the area. She had also noticed me and I became her dancing partner throughout the festival.'

At this moment Huldbrand felt a sharp pain in his left hand: with an angry look on her face Undine had bitten his fingers with her pearly teeth.

'Bertalda was friendly towards me and in jest I asked her to give me one of her gloves. "Only if you bring me a report of what it's like in the notorious forest," she said. And although I was not particularly keen on obtaining her glove, I kept my promise.

'As I was riding into the forest it occurred to me how easy it was to get lost there. As I glanced up I saw something black amongst the branches of a tall oak tree. Then suddenly it said something in a rough human voice and frightened my horse, which dashed off out of control. And just as it was about to plunge into a rocky chasm, it seemed to me that a long white man put himself in the path of the stallion, which came to a halt terrified. When I had him under control again I realised that it was not a long white man but a silvery bright stream that came rushing down from a hill nearby.'

Here Undine clapped her hands and exclaimed, 'Thank you, dear stream!'

'Hardly had I regained my position in the saddle however when a strange ugly little man appeared at my side, all brownish-yellow with a nose as big as the rest of his body. I was about to set off back home when the little man sprang in front of my horse and asked me to give him a tip for saving it. Although this was not true I dropped a gold coin into the cap he was holding out. As I galloped off it seemed to me that the green earth below me became transparent like glass and below it I could see a horde of goblins tumbling around and playing with pieces of silver and gold. My ugly companion was there and when he showed the others the coin I had given him they all fell about laughing. Then they all started to stretch out their sharp little fingers up towards me, and in horror I spurred on my horse and dashed off into the forest again.

'I wanted to follow a particular path which I believed would lead me back to the city, but an indistinct white face with constantly changing features kept blocking my way. It only let us go one way, away from the footpath. It seemed as though the face was on top of a long white body, which at times looked like a fountain that wandered around. And so finally I came out of the forest and found your little hut, and then the white man disappeared.'

When discussion turned to Huldbrand's departure, Undine started to giggle, and said, 'Just try to leave! You won't get over the stream!' Huldbrand and the old man went to see if Undine was right, and sure enough it was clear that he would have to stay on that little spit of land which had now become an island until the flood subsided.

As they went back into the hut Undine said to the knight in a surly way, 'If I hadn't bitten you, who knows what else you would have said about Bertalda!'

The old couple had come to accept the intimacy between the two young people. Huldbrand also began to feel that he was already Undine's husband and he no longer thought very much of his former life.

One evening, when the two men were drinking wine together, they suddenly heard a light knocking at the door, which frightened them all. The knocking was repeated and accompanied by a deep groan, which made Huldbrand reach for his sword. Undine approached the door and called out, 'If you're up to some mischief, Earth Spirits, then Kühleborn will teach you better!' This made the others even more afraid. But suddenly a voice outside said, 'I'm not an Earth Spirit. If you are god-fearing and want to help me, please let me in.' Undine opened the door and revealed an old priest who was obviously shocked at seeing such a marvellous creature in a small hut.

The old priest was dripping wet and dry clothes were immediately found for him. After he had been supplied with some food and wine he started to tell how he had set off the day before from the monastery on the other side of the lake to visit the local bishop. He eventually found himself swept ashore on their little island.

Huldbrand finally turned to the priest and explained to him that he and Undine were a couple, and that, if the old man and woman had nothing against it, he wanted the priest to marry them that very evening. The old couple were at first shocked but after further discussion and when the priest had satisfied himself that all parties were willing, it was agreed they should marry. The old woman went to prepare the wedding chamber and brought out two consecrated candles for the wedding ceremony. Huldbrand attempted to remove two rings from his golden chain, but noticing this Undine dashed out the door and came back with two precious rings in her hands. She explained that they had been given to her by her parents and sewn into her dress with strict instruction not to remove them until the day of her wedding. And so the wedding took place.

After the ceremony the priest said that he felt it strange that, although they had told him there was nobody else on the island, he had seen, while he was performing the rites, the imposing figure of a long man in a white cloak looking in through the window opposite him. Everyone shuddered when he suggested they might let him in and Huldbrand persuaded the priest that he must have made a mistake.

During the wedding ceremony Undine had behaved most demurely, but as soon as it was over, she teased everybody, the priest included, who finally told her that she should learn to attune her soul to that of her husband. Undine laughed at him and said, 'Soul! What if you don't have a soul, like me?' This greatly saddened the priest. Then eventually Undine herself broke into tears and said to the priest, 'A soul must be something really lovely but also terrible. Wouldn't it be better never to have one?' Everyone in the hut moved away from her shuddering. Finally the priest turned to the Knight and warned him that while there seemed to be nothing evil about her, he should take care, love her and be faithful.

Turning to Undine Huldbrand asked her what she had meant when she had talked of Earth Spirits and Kühleborn? Laughing, and in her usual light-hearted way, she said, 'Just fairy tales! Fairy tales for children! It's all over with our wedding night!'

'No it isn't,' said Huldbrand, overcome with love, and extinguishing the candles he carried his beloved into their wedding chamber.

The young married couple were wakened by the fresh light of morning. Whenever Huldbrand had fallen asleep during the night he had been disturbed by horrible dreams about ghosts who attempted to disguise themselves as beautiful women and about beautiful women who suddenly acquired the faces of dragons. But when he was fully awake he realised that Undine could have no bad intentions towards him. Huldbrand joined the old couple and the priest who were sitting by the hearth. Finally Undine appeared and everyone looked at her in amazement: she looked so strange and yet so familiar. When the priest raised his hand to bless her, she sank to her knees and begged him for forgiveness for all the stupid things she had said the day before.

Towards evening Undine led Huldbrand out to the bank of the stream, which had now lost all traces of its former wildness. She asked him to carry her across to the small island where he had found her again on that first evening. When they had settled down she began to tell him about herself:

'You must understand that there are beings who exist in the elements but only rarely let themselves be seen by you. In lakes, rivers and streams live all kinds of water spirits, which are more beautiful than humans. Many a fisherman has seen them and humans call them Undines. But you, my dear friend, can see before you a real Undine.

'But we have no souls. However, everything wants to rise above its natural state and so my father, a powerful water prince in the Mediterranean Sea, wanted his only daughter to acquire a soul. But our kind can only gain a soul through the most intimate union of love with one of your race. And now I have a soul thanks to you. If you reject me I shall plunge into this stream, which is my uncle.'

She wanted to say more but Huldbrand embraced her and carried her back to the bank. He promised never to leave her.


The following morning Huldbrand expressed the opinion that they should stay a few days longer, but Undine persuaded him that if they did so it would be only more painful for the old couple eventually. The priest agreed to accompany them, and, amid tearful farewells, they crossed over the bed of the forest stream which had now completely dried up.

The three travellers had reached the darkest part of the forest. Huldbrand and Undine rode along with only eyes for each other, and it was some time before they noticed that the priest was in conversation with a fourth traveller who had joined them. He wore a white garment similar to the priest's but with a hood that hung low over his face. The two men introduced themselves. 'I'm Pater Heilmann, from the Mariagruss Monastery on the other side of the lake,' said the priest. 'And my name is Kühleborn,' said the stranger, 'and I have something to tell the young woman there.' Suddenly he appeared on the other side of the priest next to Undine. She was terrified and wanted nothing to do with him, but he only laughed and said, 'Don't you know your uncle Kühleborn who brought you here on his back? The priest thought he'd seen me before, and he was right, because it was I who saved him from the water.' Undine begged Kühleborn to leave them, but when he showed reluctance Huldbrand leaped to her side swinging his sword at Kühleborn's head. But as he did so, it seemed that he was striking into a waterfall which came frothing down from a high cliff nearby with a loud splash and drenched them making a sound like laughter.

Soon however they were out in the open again, with the imperial city gleaming before them in the evening sun, and drying the travellers' drenched clothes.

The young knight had been greatly missed in the imperial city. When news spread of the bad storms and floods it was difficult to doubt that he had perished, and Bertalda too regretted having sent him on the fateful mission. Her foster parents had come to fetch her but she persuaded them to stay until they had certain news of the Knight.

When Huldbrand finally returned everyone was overjoyed, except Bertalda, when she saw the wonderfully beautiful wife he had brought with him. However she gradually came to accept the situation and was very friendly towards Undine. Most people took Undine for a princess, but whenever she was asked about her origins she avoided answering. The priest's lips were sealed and he soon went back to his monastery.

All three got on so well that there was soon talk of Bertalda accompanying them back to Burg Ringstetten near the source of the Danube for a while.

Everyone sat around the lunch table on Bertalda's nameday, with her at the head surrounded by all her gifts, jewellery and flowers. When the dessert was handed round the doors were left open, following the old custom, to let the common people watch them eat, and they too were allowed to share in the wine and cakes. Finally several people asked Undine to sing them a song, and she did so willingly, taking up her lute.

The song was about a child found on a shore, who was discovered by a noble duke riding by. The duke took the child to his castle and brought her up, providing her with every-thing he could, though there was one thing he could never give her. The song brought tears to the eyes of Bertalda's foster parents, the Duke and Duchess, who recognised the story of how Bertalda had been found. The Duke added, 'We were never able to give you the best thing of all.' Then Undine continued with another song about the sadness and sense of loss of the child's real parents.

Bertalda too was in tears and she begged Undine to tell her where her true parents were, and Undine indicated the figures of the old Fisherman and his wife who came staggering out of the crowd of people watching. Full of tears and praising God they embraced their long-lost daughter.

But horrified and angry Bertalda tore herself away from their embrace. She had been hoping that she was to be even more highly ennobled. She condemned Undine as a deceiver. But Undine declared that she had not been lying and that she had been told the story by the same person who had tempted Bertalda away from her parents and later put her in the path of the Duke. Finally the Duchess insisted that they know the truth before they leave, and then the old Fisherman's wife stepped forward, and bowing low before the Duchess, she said, 'If this angry young woman is my daughter, then she will have a birthmark shaped like a violet between her shoulders and a similar one on the instep of her left foot. If she would come with me…' 'I will not expose myself in front of a peasant woman,' said Bertalda, turning her back on her proudly. 'But in front of me you will,' responded the Duchess very seriously. And she took Bertalda together with the old woman into a nearby room. After a while the women returned, with Bertalda as white as a ghost. The Duchess declared that the old woman had been right and that Bertalda was indeed her daughter. Everyone left the dining area and Undine sank tearfully into Huldbrand's arms.

It was decided to leave the old city as soon as possible. As Huldbrand was taking Undine out to a coach for the journey, they were approached by a young woman selling fish. It was Bertalda who had been turned out by the Duke and Duchess, though not without a substantial dowry. The old Fisherman and his wife had also been well rewarded and returned to their home. They had told Bertalda that she should make her way dressed as a fishmaid through the infamous forest to prove herself to them. Undine took pity on her and invited her to come with them to Ringstetten. Huldbrand agreed with his wife's suggestion and said he would inform the Fisherman and his wife of their decision. And so all three set off together leaving their sad memories behind them.

On their arrival one fine evening at Burg Ringstetten, Undine and Bertalda went for a walk together along the high ramparts of the castle. She decided that she should tell Bertalda the whole story about her origins, and as she did so Bertalda began to feel that she was living in a fairy tale.

After a long time living together in Burg Ringstetten, Huldbrand found that his feelings were beginning to turn away from Undine and towards Bertalda. And during this time all kinds of ghostly figures started to appear in the vaulted corridors of the castle. The long white figure of a man making threatening gestures appeared often to both Huldbrand and Bertalda, but especially to Bertalda.

One day, when Huldbrand had gone out for a ride, Undine had the household servants bring a huge stone to cover up the well that stood in the castle yard. At first they protested that they would then have to haul up the water from down in the valley, but she persuaded them. When Bertalda found out what they were doing she ordered them to stop, because the water from the well was so good for her skin. But Undine insisted that she, as the Knight's wife, should decide such things. When the stone had finally been heaved into place, Undine leaned over it and made a mysterious inscription on it.

When Huldbrand returned Undine explained to him why she had covered the well. Whenever her uncle Kühleborn perceived that Huldbrand was unhappy with her behaviour and that this pleased Bertalda, he would come out of the well and haunt them. Huldbrand realised that Undine's intentions were well-meant and allowed the stone to stay on the well. Undine then warned him never to become angry with her when they were near water of some kind, because then her relatives would gain power over her and force her to return to living with them. Bertalda however was most unhappy at having her will thwarted, and when she did not appear for supper, a servant found a letter from her in her apartment. She wrote that she felt ashamed and realised that she was only a poor fishmaid and would return to the hut of her poor parents.

Undine urged Huldbrand to find Bertalda and stop her. And Huldbrand immediately made inquiries about where she had gone. When Undine heard that her husband had set off towards the dark valley called Schwarztal she shouted, 'Oh, don't go to the Schwarztal, not that way!' But she realised that all her shouting was in vain and she set off after him.

While Huldbrand was searching the forest in the Schwarztal for Bertalda, he was haunted by many ghostly apparitions, but eventually with Undine's help all three managed to escape.

Everything was calm and peaceful in the castle after the events in the Schwarztal and Huldbrand recognised more and more the good qualities of his wife. And so winter passed and spring came again. Huldbrand talked of how beautiful the city of Vienna was and how wonderful it was to travel along the Danube. Bertalda expressed the wish to undertake such a journey and Undine was also enthusiastic about it.

But they had only been on the Danube for a few days when Kühleborn started to show the extent of his powers again. Hardly had they closed their eyes at night when everybody on the ship became aware of a horrible human head that rose up vertically out of the waves and accompanied the vessel on its way. Soon all the water around the ship was teeming with the most terrifying shapes. Only when Undine woke up did they all disappear.

Then, one evening, Bertalda was sitting by the edge of the ship. She had undone a golden necklace given to her by Huldbrand and was playing with it over the surface of the water and enjoying the way it reflected the evening light. Suddenly a huge hand reached up out of the Danube, grasped the necklace and disappeared again under the water. Bertalda cried out and Huldbrand could finally control his temper no longer. Undine begged him not to scold her while they were on the water. She dipped her hand into water and brought up a marvellously beautiful coral necklace which she offered to Bertalda. But Huldbrand tore the ornament from her hand and hurled it back into the river. He shouted at her in a rage: 'You're still in league with them, so stay with them and leave us human beings alone!' Undine wept like a hurt child: 'Oh, dear friend, remain faithful to me. Then I can protect you from them. But now, because of what you have done, I must leave you!' And she slipped off the ship and seemed to fade away into the waters of the Danube.

Huldbrand lay on the deck in tears and soon became unconscious.

For a long time Huldbrand remained inconsolable for the loss of Undine, and she came to him often in dreams, though less and less as time went by. Then one day the old Fisherman appeared at the castle, having heard of Undine's disappearance, and demanded that Bertalda now return to her true home, as it was not honourable to live with a man who had lost his wife. However, Huldbrand's affection for Bertalda had increased and he now wanted to marry her, but, as the old man pointed out, they could not be sure if Undine was really dead. Nevertheless the change in heart that he perceived in Bertalda finally persuaded him to allow the marriage. And the old priest Pater Heilmann was sent for.

Over the last fourteen nights Undine had appeared to the priest in his dreams, sobbing and begging him: 'Stop him, dear Father! I'm still alive! Save his body! Save his soul!' And so the priest had come, not to join the couple together but to keep them apart. But the couple refused to heed the priest's warning and he left the castle. The next morning Huldbrand sent for another priest who promised to consecrate their marriage a few days later.

Then one night Huldbrand had a strange dream. It seemed as though a flock of singing swans was transporting him over land and sea, until one of the swans whispered to him that he was hovering over the Mediterranean Sea. The waves had become crystals and he was able to look down to the bottom of the sea where he could see Undine under the great crystal vaults. She looked very sad and was weeping. Kühleborn came up to her and scolded her, but she replied that as she had brought her soul back with her she should be allowed to weep. He replied, 'But you are also still subject to our laws and you must pass judgement on him and bring about his death, if he marries again and is unfaithful to you.' 'I have sealed the well,' said Undine. 'But if he leaves his castle or has the well opened again?' asked Kühleborn. 'That's why I arranged for him to dream about hovering over the Mediterranean and hearing our conversation,' said Undine, smiling through her tears. Kühleborn looked up angrily at the Knight and disappeared. The swans began to flap their wings gently again and transported him back home to Burg Ringstetten, where he awoke in his bed.

On the day of the wedding it seemed to everyone that the main person was missing from the celebration, Undine. And as night came, Bertalda sat looking at herself in the mirror lamenting the freckles on her neck. She sighed to her maids: 'I could get rid of them. But the well is sealed up, from which I used to obtain the water that purified my skin.' And one of her maids arranged for the stone to be removed from the well.

The men who worked at heaving the stone off the well found that it was easier than they expected. It was as though some force were helping them from within the well. As they finally rolled the stone off it, a huge column of water shot up in the form of a pale woman veiled in white. She was weeping, and wringing her hands over her head, she moved off slowly towards the main castle building. The servants fled away at the sight of her. Bertalda saw her whining below her window, but then she moved on, moving heavily, as though driven, but hesitating and as though she were going to some high court of judgement. Bertalda shouted to the servants that they should call the Knight, but no one dared to move. The strange wandering figure wandered into the castle and up the stairs.

Huldbrand was standing alone in his room in front of the mirror when there was a faint knocking on the door. He thought he was imagining it and said to himself, 'I must go to my marriage bed.' A weeping voice outside said, 'But it will be a cold one.' Then he saw the door open in the mirror and the white figure entered, closing the door behind it. Softly she said, 'They have opened the well, and now you must die.' His heart seemed to stop and he felt that there was no other way. 'But don't drive me mad in the hour of my death with some horrible visage behind that veil.' The wandering figure said, 'I am as beautiful as when you first wooed me.' Huldbrand sighed, 'If only that were true and I could die by one kiss from you.' 'Willingly,' she said. And she pushed back her veil to reveal her lovely face. Trembling with love and the imminence of death he bent towards her. She kissed him with a heavenly kiss, but did not let him go, pulling him closer and weeping as though she wanted to weep away her soul. Her tears entered his eyes and moved in sweet waves through his breast, until he breathed his last and sank back on the bed as a corpse.

To the servants in the antechamber she said, 'I wept him to death,' and walked slowly back to the well.

Pater Heilmann arrived at the castle as soon as news spread about Huldbrand's death, and attempted to comfort his bride, who called Undine a murderess and sorceress. The old Fisherman however took a calmer view and saw it as the judgement of God, and was of the opinion that no one had suffered more from Huldbrand's death than poor Undine herself. He helped to organise the funeral, and Huldbrand was buried with his ancestors as the last in his line.

In the middle of the funeral service there suddenly appeared a white deeply veiled figure amongst the black-clothed mourners. The figure moved through the mourners till it was just behind Bertalda. When they reached the open grave Bertalda noticed the figure and, partly in anger, partly in fear, she asked her to leave the area. The veiled figure shook its head and seemed to be beseeching Bertalda, who was moved by memories of Undine's good intentions. After the burial ceremony was completed it was noticed that the white figure had disappeared, and from the spot where it had been kneeling, there gushed now a silvery bright spring that continued to flow until it had almost surrounded the knight's grave. Then it flowed on into a small pond at the side of the graveyard.

And still, many years later, the villagers pointed to the spring and said it was the poor rejected Undine embracing her lover.

# BIOGRAPHICAL NOTES

Nigel Bryant worked for many years as a theatre director and radio drama producer for the BBC, and is very interested in the oral nature of medieval literature, that it was intended primarily for performance, for reading aloud. His translations from medieval French include *The High Book of the Grail* (the thirteenth-century romance *Perlesvaus*), Chrétien de Troyes' *Perceval* and its continuations, Robert de Boron's trilogy *Merlin and the Grail*, a compilation of all the major Grail romances entitled *The Legend of the Grail*, the *True Chronicles of Jean le Bel 1290–1360*, and the fourteenth-century *Perceforest: the Prehistory of King Arthur's Britain*.

Dr Ann Lawson Lucas was Senior Lecturer in Italian at the University of Hull. Mainly published in Italy, her books concern nineteenth-century writers for young people, especially Emilio Salgari (1862–1911), the leading writer of adventure novels. She is the translator and editor of Carlo Collodi's *The Adventures of Pinocchio* (Oxford World's Classics). She is a life Fellow of the International Research Society for Children's Literature, on behalf of which she founded the scholarly journal, *International Research in Children's Literature* (Edinburgh University Press).

Dr David Carter has taught at St Andrews and Southampton universities in the UK and has been Professor of Communicative English at Yonsei University, Seoul. His PhD.was on Freud's theories of creativity and aesthetics and he has taught on Freud and Jung, and also on the German Romantics, the brothers Grimm and the 'Märchen' tradition. He has published on psychoanalysis, literature, drama, film history and applied linguistics, is also a freelance journalist and translator, and has published books on the Belgian author Georges Simenon and Literary Theory, as well as in the field of film studies, the most recent being *East Asian Cinema* and *The Western*. For Hesperus he has written *Brief Lives: Honoré de Balzac*, *Brief Lives: Sigmund Freud* and *Brief Lives: Marquis de Sade*. He has also translated Balzac's 'Sarrasine', Georges Simenon's *Three Crimes*, Klaus Mann's *Alexander* and Sigmund Freud's *On Cocaine*, and other works.

## HESPERUS PRESS

Hesperus Press is committed to bringing near what is far –
far both in space and time. Works written by the greatest
authors, and unjustly neglected or simply little known in
the English-speaking world, are made accessible through
new translations and a completely fresh editorial approach.
Through these classic works, the reader is introduced to the
greatest writers from all times and all cultures.

For more information on Hesperus Press, please visit our
website: **www.hesperuspress.com**

## SELECTED TITLES FROM HESPERUS PRESS

| Author | Title | Foreword writer |
|---|---|---|
| Pietro Aretino | *The School of Whoredom* | Paul Bailey |
| Pietro Aretino | *The Secret Life of Nuns* | |
| Jane Austen | *Lesley Castle* | Zoë Heller |
| Jane Austen | *Love and Friendship* | Fay Weldon |
| Honoré de Balzac | *Colonel Chabert* | A.N. Wilson |
| Charles Baudelaire | *On Wine and Hashish* | Margaret Drabble |
| Giovanni Boccaccio | *Life of Dante* | A.N. Wilson |
| Charlotte Brontë | *The Spell* | |
| Emily Brontë | *Poems of Solitude* | Helen Dunmore |
| Mikhail Bulgakov | *Fatal Eggs* | Doris Lessing |
| Mikhail Bulgakov | *The Heart of a Dog* | A.S. Byatt |
| Giacomo Casanova | *The Duel* | Tim Parks |
| Miguel de Cervantes | *The Dialogue of the Dogs* | Ben Okri |
| Geoffrey Chaucer | *The Parliament of Birds* | |
| Anton Chekhov | *The Story of a Nobody* | Louis de Bernières |
| Anton Chekhov | *Three Years* | William Fiennes |
| Wilkie Collins | *The Frozen Deep* | |
| Joseph Conrad | *Heart of Darkness* | A.N. Wilson |
| Joseph Conrad | *The Return* | Colm Tóibín |
| Gabriele D'Annunzio | *The Book of the Virgins* | Tim Parks |
| Dante Alighieri | *The Divine Comedy: Inferno* | |
| Dante Alighieri | *New Life* | Louis de Bernières |
| Daniel Defoe | *The King of Pirates* | Peter Ackroyd |
| Marquis de Sade | *Incest* | Janet Street-Porter |
| Charles Dickens | *The Haunted House* | Peter Ackroyd |
| Charles Dickens | *A House to Let* | |
| Fyodor Dostoevsky | *The Double* | Jeremy Dyson |
| Fyodor Dostoevsky | *Poor People* | Charlotte Hobson |
| Alexandre Dumas | *One Thousand and One Ghosts* | |

| | | |
|---|---|---|
| Francis Petrarch | *My Secret Book* | Germaine Greer |
| Luigi Pirandello | *Loveless Love* | |
| Edgar Allan Poe | *Eureka* | Sir Patrick Moore |
| Alexander Pope | *The Rape of the Lock and A Key to the Lock* | Peter Ackroyd |
| Antoine-François Prévost | *Manon Lescaut* | Germaine Greer |
| Marcel Proust | *Pleasures and Days* | A.N. Wilson |
| Alexander Pushkin | *Dubrovsky* | Patrick Neate |
| Alexander Pushkin | *Ruslan and Lyudmila* | Colm Tóibín |
| François Rabelais | *Pantagruel* | Paul Bailey |
| François Rabelais | *Gargantua* | Paul Bailey |
| Christina Rossetti | *Commonplace* | Andrew Motion |
| George Sand | *The Devil's Pool* | Victoria Glendinning |
| Jean-Paul Sartre | *The Wall* | Justin Cartwright |
| Friedrich von Schiller | *The Ghost-seer* | Martin Jarvis |
| Mary Shelley | *Transformation* | |
| Percy Bysshe Shelley | *Zastrozzi* | Germaine Greer |
| Stendhal | *Memoirs of an Egotist* | Doris Lessing |
| Robert Louis Stevenson | *Dr Jekyll and Mr Hyde* | Helen Dunmore |
| Theodor Storm | *The Lake of the Bees* | Alan Sillitoe |
| Leo Tolstoy | *The Death of Ivan Ilych* | |
| Leo Tolstoy | *Hadji Murat* | Colm Tóibín |
| Ivan Turgenev | *Faust* | Simon Callow |
| Mark Twain | *The Diary of Adam and Eve* | John Updike |
| Mark Twain | *Tom Sawyer, Detective* | |
| Oscar Wilde | *The Portrait of Mr W.H.* | Peter Ackroyd |
| Virginia Woolf | *Carlyle's House and Other Sketches* | Doris Lessing |
| Virginia Woolf | *Monday or Tuesday* | Scarlett Thomas |
| Emile Zola | *For a Night of Love* | A.N. Wilson |